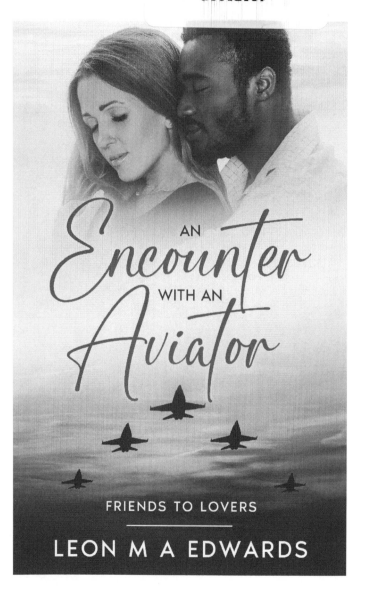

An Encounter
WITH AN
Aviator

FRIENDS TO LOVERS

LEON M A EDWARDS

Time Away

♥

I'm reviewing a PowerPoint presentation on my laptop in my office before a board meeting in 30 minutes.

Each year, I deliver a speech assessing the management of every department.

I work for a corporate business that occupies multiple floors of a skyscraper and has a workforce of five hundred employees.

Its location is in central Los Angeles.

In my office, I'm going through my PowerPoint presentation before a board meeting. During my review, a board member tells me it's time.

I request them to be patient and close the application on my laptop while I grab my suit jacket to head into the boardroom.

My colleague walks beside me while wearing a concerned expression, questioning if I'm alright. I'm not attentive and can't concentrate on what I'll say at the meeting.

It is unsurprising to see their gazes when I enter the room. It's not my power suit, corporate tie and crisp clean shirt that is drawing their attention. My unkept appearance is something they are not accustomed to.

I've let my hair and beard grow without any grooming. My appearance leans towards grunge rather than conservative.

They are sitting around the board table waiting for me to present my slides.

I am struggling to focus on my meeting, personal life and appointment schedule at the same time. My heart is racing and I'm struggling to connect my laptop to the projector due to my clumsy fingers. My various commitments are getting on top of me, and I can't seem to keep focused.

The presence of multiple pairs of eyes is not aiding me, causing me to lose my place at the start of my presentation. It shouldn't be a problem since they all work for me and I should feel comfortable in front of my employees. I feel overwhelmed with nerves, losing control and struggling to think clearly.

While I'm getting anxious, a colleague approaches me and I give a nervous laugh as I look into her eyes. She gestures for me to end the meeting. I fight to resume the execution of my PowerPoint slides, but I'm awkwardly pulled out of the boardroom.

The presentation is taken over quickly by someone else.

While the presentation continues, I go back to my office.

I'm told it is finally time to take leave of absent. I haven't taken a day off in 4.5 years and I'm close to burnout.

I'll entrust my team to handle the business during my sabbatical leave.

There was a planned intervention after the meeting which I was not made of aware of at the time.

Someone packed my luggage from my home. They had taken it to my office, during the board meeting, implying I need to leave.

I seek reassurance regarding the company's management by asking my secretary to call my daughter into my office.

A lot of paperwork and appointments need attention and need someone to take care of both.

I wonder what took place in the meeting upon returning to the office. I disliked a junior staff telling me to take leave and thinking they know what's best for me. I own the damn company. Built it from the ground up.

While I'm mad, I bring up pictures of my late wife on my laptop, which is on a time loop. Photos of us together and on her own. Watching how she used to smile while I rest my chin against the back of my hands on the desk.

Just staring at the screen, watching the media going round in a loop.

Someone appears at my glass door and notice it is one of my daughters. She works at the company as a normal employee with no board management position. She is a supervisor and learning the ropes so she and her sister can run the business at some point in future.

I wonder if she or her sister were a part of the coo to have me take a break from work and ask, 'Shona, was you and your sisters apart of making me take absent of leave?'

Shona appears guilty with her hands in her pockets, deflecting the question as she asks, 'How are you? I heard you were asked to step down for a while.'

I don't hide my thoughts and say, 'I'm angry. Some knot kid who works for me tells me to leave the room. Then I come into my office to see a luggage packed.'

Shona tries not to smile while trying to show sympathy and says, 'You will always own the company. It is not a public company. You are the sole director on the paperwork. There will be no hostile take over while you go away.'

I trust the company will be in good hands but I say, 'I need to work. If I stop... all I will have left are the memories of your mother. I need to work to distract me from dwelling on your mother not being here.'

Shona sits on one of the chairs in front of my desk and says, 'It's called grieving. What you are ignoring is allowing yourself to accepts mom has gone. You need time to grieve. You haven't started. It has been five years and all you have done is buried yourself in work. Not even taking care of yourself. When did you last eat a good meal?'

I deflect the question and say, 'Work is busy. I've had to secure a lot of work to keep the company afloat.'

Shona scoffs and says, 'The company had already tripled its income. We did not need the additional business to stay afloat. Go. And don't come back until you have let go of mom.'

I have no intention of letting go and say, 'Your mother will never be forgotten. She was my north, south, east, and west. She gave me a reason to create this company. She encouraged me to fulfill my dream of being my own boss.'

Shona makes herself clear by saying, 'I didn't imply you forget about her. I meant to move on. We have. It's what mom would have wanted.'

I sit back and tap the tip of my fingers on the desk and say, 'Well, I can't.'

Shona has one more thing to say, 'I miss the old you. You don't look like yourself with the grunge look. You used to be clean shaven and a clean haircut.'

Nothing else is said and my daughter leaves my office to myself. I spend another twenty minutes staring at the luggage as I wonder where I can go.

Leaving could be a good idea since I'm stuck in a loop and wishing for my old life back with my wife.

Begrudgingly, I go along with what I was advised and walk over to the suitcase.

I have no idea how long my employees are expecting me to be away. I'm uncertain if this will work as I feel I'm running away from my problem of not letting ago. All I will be doing is giving my loss a holiday. Moving my aching heart to another part of America will not stop the feeling I have of pining for my wife.

To delay leaving, I open the suitcase to see if I need additional things like toiletry, underwear and clothes. While I'm going through my things I wonder where I should go. My social life is not very active due to a lack of friends and places to visit. I rack my brain to think of where to go. It's been over five years since my last vacation.

As I zip up the suitcase after checking it, I recall a friend from high school I've not seen in years. He was able to get my company to insure a fleet of fighter jets at his naval base, in *Fallon*.

There was an open-ended offer to go visit him. I wonder if that offer was genuine or out of politeness. It's been a long time since I saw him and wonder it will be a good idea to stay with him and his family.

I go over to my desk to search for his personal number in my cell phone. Once I find it in my contact list, I nervously text him to ask how he has been and if I could come to see him. I wait thinking I could be sat in my office all evening waiting for a reply.

Almost instantly, my cell phone pings with a welcome response. It is the response I wanted asking when and how long. I reply with a question mark suggesting now. Hoping he will say yes at short notice, he replies allowing me to come over now.

I close my eyes with relief. I give him an open ended stay and happy to find a hotel but his text tells me I can stay at his place.

Not sure what I'm expected to do with the free time as I have no hobbies or interests unless it is making a business deal. Now I'm not working, I wonder what I do with my idle mind. There are only so many restaurants, coffee shops and shopping malls you can go to.

Knowing I have somewhere to go, I call my secretary to ready the private jet to fly me over. It is too far to be driving all that way across the Nevada state.

When my secretary comes back to me confirming when the private jet will be ready to take me, I ask her to get a limousine we hire from to take me to the private airfield.

My old school friend lives on a base called *Fallon Station* in *Nevada* about six and half hours drive from *Las Vegas*.

The last I remember is he works on a navy air base as a pilot instructor for up and coming missions which require knowledge of the area and specific skills.

It makes me smile knowing he works at a place where a movie was made to portrait what they do. It is true what they nick name the base. *Top Gun.*

It will feel weird bumping into real fighter pilots again and watching them take off and land. Maybe my friend will take me up in one of them. Probably make me feel sick taking sharp turns and loop to loops.

Six months have passed, and I have spent the time going for walks when home alone instead of staring at four walls. He and his family have treated me like one of their own. Having dinner with them every night and hearing them making small talk. I have kept to myself all this time, not opening up very much. Been making empty small talk about my day and nothing about my background, except I work in insurance. But, they think I'm employed.

They are a great family who remind me of how my family is where they sit down for dinner and talk about how their days have been. The family is unintrusive and gives me the space to allow me to open up when I'm ready.

I'm giving free rein to their house and food as well as paying my way by transferring money to their bank account. I plan on making a final healthy payment deposit when I'm ready to go home to show my appreciation.

I've been spending my time go to the navy gym and taking walks to get my bearings around the place. Occasionally I have been going to the coffee shop to people watch and see how together their lives are. Wishing my life was theirs, so I wouldn't have these emotional pains.

I have also been going for jogs inside and outside the naval base compound. To find something to do and take my mind away from being a widow. I cannot stand still as it will cause me to dwell on the past and face my feelings of loss. I prefer to keep burying those thoughts.

Tonight, the house will be empty with the kids going out with their friends and the parents are out on a date night. So, for the first time, I'm going to find a bar for the night. Staying home alone does not appeal to me.

I'm thinking of heading back in four weeks time. So, spend the remaining time seeing what is around here.

My friend gave me a choice of bars to go within walking distance, so I do not need to worry about driving.

I choose to go to the bar, which is a five-minute walk. I have been warned it is a popular venue due to being a stone's throw away from residence homes.

It has only gone five o'clock and so I watch a show I stream on television until it is time to get ready and go. While the show is playing, I hear everyone running around getting ready on their night out.

I will wait for them to leave before I get changed.

After they have all left for the evening, I go change and afterwards see myself in the mirror. I wonder whether I should shave and cut my hair. I have not touched my facial hair or my hair on top for over five years. It is what I'm used to seeing now. But, I prefer to keep my appearance until I can finally get busy living again rather than stay stuck in the past.

When I'm ready to leave, I feel nervous going out in public socializing.

Going out exercising did not involve interacting with anyone else or having to make conversation with someone else.

This time, I assume I will be approached and expected to make conversation.

Hoping I can have a drink in peace and not be interrupted.

As I make my way to the bar, a part of me wants to walk back and stay in with a bottle of wine to keep me company. Not sure if I really want to venture out among strangers or be alone.

I turn round to walk back for a few steps. Then turn round to face the direction of the bar. Hesitant to make my mind up to make myself go out.

My rational side is telling me to step out of my comfort zone despite my emotions.

First Night Out

♥

I'm Ethan Taylor, a black man in my forties. My height is six feet five inches and I have a slender, athletic build from working out at the gym.

My hair is typically grade zero, and I keep a clean-shaven look.

If the bar is shabby, my homeless look will blend in perfectly. Going to an elegant bar will result in odd stares.

Normally I wear two-piece suits socially with a casual shirt, but today I'm wearing slim-fitted jeans, a slim-fitted T-shirt, and loafers.

Since becoming a widow, I haven't been interested in anyone else and don't think I ever will be. None of the girls around here have caught my eye.

I have no plans to hurry and meet someone. Chances of meeting someone out here are slim. So, I will not have to worry about making myself fall for another woman. I would feel like I'm betraying my wife's memory by doing that. I occasionally speak to her as if she's present, seeking her guidance. It's mostly about how to handle my daughters when they're driving me insane.

Her voice echoes in my mind, urging me to be patient and reminding me that being a single parent is challenging.

I cannot imagine being with someone else, which makes it hard for me to talk to my wife and continue our relationship.

That's why I haven't been able to move on and grieve properly.

The weather is warm tonight, and it's not yet dark. I can feel the warm breeze on my arm. Fighter jets can still be heard taking off in the distance, with their lights flashing on the wings.

It seems like everyone has already arrived at their social event while I'm the only one taking a stroll. The place feels like a deserted caravan park.

I keep company by engaging in conversation with my wife.

I finally arrived at the bar after a few minutes of walking. It is not what I thought it would be. The exterior of the place is painted in a fresh light green color that makes it appear less gloomy. I want to see inside to see if it will be to my liking.

The customers appear to be the type of people I would get along with and decide to go inside.

Wide window panels in the bar allow you to see how busy it is inside. There is a glass door to walk through and you hear the noise as soon as you walk in. Their uniform immediately tells me that the patrons are navy personnel. I think I'm the only civilian in here.

There's a rectangle-shaped bar at the center of the place with curved corners. The wood is a solid dark brown, and it's encircled by a brass railing. The stools are placed at irregular intervals.

I notice an empty space at the bar and wait for service.

An elderly man owns the bar and his niece assists whenever possible, in addition to her work schedule. This evening, she's serving drinks while her uncle replaces a barrel in the cellar.

Pamela Gray is a Caucasian woman in her mid-forties with brown hair that falls below her shoulders, which she ties back tightly into a bun at the back of her head. She has on jean shorts, a navy blue vest and white trainers. She has a friendly, platonic relationship with the regulars at the bar.

Her job has given her a naturally athletic body and dark olive skin from being in the sun.

Dark brown eyes and a cute smile accentuate her flawless face.

She has a limited family, consisting of her uncle and two sisters. Her parents are no longer alive,and her uncle played a role in raising all three of them. In hopes of finding more lucrative careers, her two sisters left the town. They occasionally visit Pamela and vice versa.

She's currently unattached, and her last romantic involvement was during her teenage years, years ago. Putting her career first, she reached great heights, causing men to feel threatened by her success. Finding a relationship has been a challenge, and being turned down for someone else has affected her confidence. She's resolved to the fact that she won't ever find a husband.

When referring to her, friends and colleagues use the name Pam.

As I wait to be served, I feel uneasy being the only one here with a scruffy look while everyone else has a clean shave and trendy hairstyle.

After some time, the bartender approaches and I realize I find her attractive without much contemplation. She waits for me to indicate my beverage choice.

I get tongue tied as I have no idea what brand of beer to buy and say, 'Uh. What do you have?'

Indicating the draft taps, she recites the different drinks.

I glance over at the labels, playing it safe and say, 'I'll go for the Budweiser.'

She grabs a glass from above her and spins it in her hand before pouring out the beer. After filling the glass, she introduces herself and asks where I am from.

I find her name is sweet and say, 'From Los Angeles.'

I get my cell phone and open the wallet app with my bank card details stored with contactless. I'm at the point where I'm ready to pay for my drink.

Pam hands over the card machine with a quizzical expression and says, 'You're a long way from home. What are you doing here?'

I tap my cell phone over the card machine and don't go into detail when I say, 'Staying with a friend. First time out for a night. He is out with his wife for their anniversary. So, decided to go for a drink instead of staring at four walls.'

Pam stares at my appearance and says, 'You don't seem like a bum or out of work.'

I wonder how she knows and ask, 'What makes you think I'm not homeless? I could have come here and found a floor to sleep on until I get to my feet.'

Pam glances at my watch and says, 'That is a big giveaway. How can someone like you afford a watch like that if you were homeless? And your clothes are nice for a poor person to afford. Who are you staying with?'

I'm vague about my friend I've been staying with and say, 'Someone I know lives out here. I've been staying at his place for six months. His family has been, let's say, patience putting up with my mood swings and giving me leeway.'

Pam wonders I do for work and asks, 'What do you do?'

I take a gulp of beer and say, 'I'm an actuary.'

Cheering noise in the background made it difficult for her to hear what I said.

Pam doesn't hear me properly and guesses by asking, 'An aviator?'

I smile, almost laughing at the idea, and correct her by saying, 'No. An actuary. I don't think the navy would accept my appearance if I was a pilot.'

Pam quietly laughs with the most beautiful smile I have not seen in a while and says, 'Obviously. I thought you were going to impress me by saying you were a pilot. Whats with the grunge look?'

I avoid the real answer and instead say, 'I went on sabbatical leave and thought I would let my hair down. Normally, I'm clean shaven with a hair like them over there playing pool.'

Pam sees where I'm staring and says, 'Yeah. Now, they are real pilots and happen to be the best. Have you ever heard the phrase *Top Gun*?'

I smile, already knowing and say, 'You're kidding. That is real? And which one is your boyfriend?'

Pam leans over the bar and stares into my eyes before asking, 'Who says I have a thing for pilots?'

I go blank and wonder if I have offended her and say, 'I didn't mean to insult you. You are very pretty and assumed one of them would have impressed you.'

Pam is messing with me and says, 'I'm only kidding. You must have a girl back home.'

I fail to smile as I think of my wife and say, 'No. Not met the right one.'

The focus of the conversation shifts to her.

I wonder about her bar work and ask, 'How long have you been working here?'

Pam serves another person as she says, 'This is not my job. I help out my uncle.'

I'm intrigued and ask, 'What do you do for a living?'

Pam is vague when she says, 'I work on planes.'

I guess her occupation by asking, 'You're a flight attendant?'

Pam finishes serving as she says, 'Something like that.'

I ask her about her travels while I tap a sip of my beer and say, 'Have you seen a lot of the world?'

Pam has a think before saying, 'A little. Been to parts near the Indian Ocean.'

I find her life interesting and ask, 'You not met a nice pilot or another flight attendant?'

Pam nods her head and says, 'No. I don't want to meet anyone through work.'

I wonder what her type is but say, 'So, we both have not met the right one. Don't worry, you will.'

Pam is curious and asks, 'How come you are so sure?'

I have always had a gut feeling all my life and say, 'I just know. I think you will meet him in the month. It is a gift I have. I seem to be able to guess certain things.'

Pam wonders if it is why he is in insurance and asks, 'Is that why you are an actuary? Predict outcomes?'

I smile and say, 'Something like that. It made the company I work for a lot of money.'

One of the guys playing pool walks over to order a round in.

Pam seems to know him and asks, 'Hi Trojan. Another five pints?'

Trojan nods his head and asks, 'How are you? Still trying to pull a man? I don't think he is after a cougar.'

Pam shakes her head while she says, 'Very funny. We are just having a friendly chat. What about what her face?'

Trojan recollects and says, 'Oh. Jessica. She crashed and burned. Couldn't keep up. When are you going to let yourself go and find someone? We are making bets you're gay. It's okay, cougar. Nothing wrong with being gay.'

Pam chuckles and hides her embarrassment as she says, 'I will find a real man when you stop being a jerk. Which will be never.'

Trojan laughs, then says, 'You won't meet anyone stuck behind the bar. I would say you are a back seat driver, but you need to be with someone to do that.'

I watch him laughing as he walks away with the drinks and says, 'Is this normal around here? You okay?'

Pam has gone red and says, 'It's okay. He can be an idiot. You want another one?'

I had not realized I had already finished my pint and say, 'Yeah. Like I said, you will meet him in the next month.'

Five pints later and at closing time, we were still conversing. I offer to help her clear up.

While placing a tray of empty glasses on the bar, I notice a picture on a cork board behind the bar. Pam walks up next to me with empty glasses and I ask her about the photo.

Pam shrugs it off and says, 'It's my dad. My uncle who you saw tonight owns this place, and he is my dads brother.'

I can see straight away he was a pilot and asked, 'Was he a casualty of war? Or was it personal?'

Pam has a glint in her eye as she stares at the picture and says, 'He was killed in action. Took three planes down before he bought it.'

I feel a sense he was a good dad and say, 'So, he did it right.'

Pam sighs as she says, 'Yeah. Kind of how I got into the industry.'

I see it as well and say, 'How long ago?'

Pam reminiscences and says, 'Twenty years ago. I was thirteen. Went a little nuts in the first year.'

I can relate to her and say, 'I know what you mean.'

Pam is curious and says, 'You lost someone?'

I realize what I said and say, 'No. I was imagining what it could be like. So, can see how you would have gone off the rails.'

Her uncle implies it's time to leave and I ask how far she lives. She's a ten-minute walk away and I offer to accompany her to ensure she gets home safely.

While we're walking, I ask her how she likes to unwind.

Pam does not do much and says, 'Just go for coffee. Go for walks. How long are you in town for Ethan?'

I have not really thought about it and say, 'will probably leave at the end of the month. Work has been calling me, asking when I will be back. Have a few loose ends.'

Pam is surprised she has not seen him around town and asks, 'Where have you been hiding?'

I smile at her question and say, 'hibernation. Been keeping to myself and driving out of town to see what is around. Clearing my head. Seeing the sights.'

It is not long before I reach her place she says is her home. There's a mix of unease and excitement in her as she tries to get inside. I take the hint and start walking towards my friend's home.

Briefing

The next day, Pam arrived for duty wearing her beige trousers and shirts, which were neatly ironed and sharp. Her papers ordered her back to *Naval Air Station Fallon*, where she graduated as a top gun fighter pilot. She was the best in her class that year. There are nine others who have been told to return, but she is unaware.

The reason for her being called on a secret mission remains unknown to her.

Ethan was misled by Pam about her occupation as a navy pilot fighting for the air force. She concealed the fact that her real home was on the base in one of the quarters from him. Also, there's no desire to meet him again.

The location for the meeting is one of the floors in one of the lecture buildings. Rows of seats face the front of the room, where there is a lecture lectern and a whiteboard for a projector. Pam must arrive by 10 o'clock and is punctual.

Upon arrival, she observes that other people are present and recognizes that they also possess the same order papers.

Through assignments and station, Pam is able to recognize the other nine pilots. She spots a free chair to take a seat on. She sits down and looks back to see their facial expressions. Just as she's about to get a reading, a man enters and walks to the front of the room. Cougar is Pam's call sign among nine others such as *Razor, Storm, Delta, Trojan, Venom, Enigma, Pulsa, Lobster, and Fox.* It wasn't used in a derogatory manner at the bar.

The nine men share the same physique, typical of pilots, and are of mixed Caucasian, black, and Asian. Pam is the sole female in the group and was requested to give up her life for their country.

America is constructing a new advanced plane with modern technology and weapons, but there's a problem. Our supply of components is from China.

The components were somehow identified for their intended use. China opted to construct their own version utilizing the same parts. The intellectual property patent has been breached, with no response from the Chinese government. The US military is against the construction of it by the Chinese military.

The location where the plane is being built has been discovered by the US, and the Chinese have pre-orders with six weeks to finish.

The admiral instructed the pilots to embark on a perilous mission, implying that they might not return. He goes by the call sign Buzz Saw and has a presentation that outlines the mission's risks and responsibilities.

The projector is turned on and an image of the building is displayed.

The factory building is constructed of brick and has a black roof. Inside, a state-of-the-art fighter jet is being built and will soon be sold to America's adversaries. A problem has arisen due to the fact that the technology and plans for the new fighter jet were stolen from an

American company in charge of its development. Being built in the wilderness, the factory can detect any threats from air or ground from miles away. The site is too far inland for tomahawks to reach from the coast. Mountains can be seen inland behind the factory, while the land is flat. There's a single entrance and exit that is regulated by security.

The *SAMs* can detect an aircraft up to six miles away and can be activated for launch within four miles.

To distract the missiles, three *F/A-18F Super Hornets* will be used to lead away the missiles and neutralise them. Two extra fighter jets will be deployed to eliminate the target. One to blow open the doors and another to destroy the content, including the plane itself.

Buzz Saw begins the presentation by saying, 'You have been called here for two reasons. You are the best of the best. But also, you have none of your own family or a long-term relationship. You are not leaving anyone a widow or orphan. As you can imagine, your papers were served to you guys. This task is a suicidal mission. The most sophisticated jet on the planet is being built and could be finished by the end of next month. It will hold our latest technology, which will be available to our enemies. When orders are made to buy the plane, all our enemies will know our hand. Any questions?'

Storm casually puts his hand up and asks, 'When do you want us to fly in?'

Buzz Saw already has a schedule and says, 'We attack the factory in six weeks. There are three challenges. The first is taking out the SAMs. The second is destroying the factory. The third is flying back in one piece.'

Cougar is baffled and says, 'I thought you said this was a suicidal mission.'

Buzz Saw still wants them to make it home and says, 'There is still a small chance of getting back. But with only your guns and counter measures. They have *Chengdu J-20's* which are faster. So, I will need to see how good you are. And train you for the attack. Starting today,

I will be testing your limits and preparing you for the assignment over the next six weeks.'

The ten of them pair off and fly in five *F18s* as they are the planes they have on *Fallon Station* to train with and Buzz Saw takes off by himself. Who they pair with is who they will fly with to complete the mission. The ten are paired together as follows.

Cougar and Storm

Pulsa and Enigma

Razor and Delta

Venom and Trojan

Fox and Lobster

Cougar, Pulsa, Razor, Venom and Fox are flying, and the rest are operating weapons systems.

Buzz Saw will conduct five separate training exercises to test everyone's skills individually. Enigma and Pulsa will be tested first, followed by Razor and Delta, Lobster and Fox, Venom and Trojan, with Cougar and Storm being last in the testing order.

As each pair takes to the sky, their fellow officers will tune in on the comms from the ground to listen during the training exercise.

Enigma and Pulsa are flying at an altitude of ten thousand feet, waiting for their instructor to join them in mid-air.

The sun is beating down on the ground on yet another sunny day with only blue skies. They are traveling at a speed of 500 miles per hour for the training exercise.

Enigma is keen to get the exercise over with and says, 'Pulsa, can you see him on the radar yet?'

Pulsa has no sign of him and says, 'Nothing yet. But I feel him close.'

Enigma wonders who this instructor is and asks, 'Do you know anything about this guy?'

Pulsa is in the dark as him and says, 'Nope. But, I guess he will be rusty. He's gotta be sixty. Probably his last order.'

Enigma agrees and says, 'What is he going to teach us what we already know? We have been dropping bombs since forever.'

Pulsa is only interested in preparing for their mission and says, 'Let's give him what he wants. Only six weeks of this.'

There is still no sign of him.

Buzz Saw flew up five minutes later, traveling at a few hundred feet below them. Traveling at six hundred miles an hour, it does not take long to catch up with them.

As he approaches them, he matches their speed by easing off the throttle and switching off the afterburners.

Buzz Saw makes communication, saying, 'This is your instructor. Bear with me as I'm a little rusty, so let's see how we get on.'

Pulsa quickly sees where he is on the radar and says, 'I can't see him.'

Enigma is on high alert and says, 'Get on it.'

Buzz Saw is directly under them and says, 'Three minutes will begin in now.'

Buzz Saw creeps behind them and switches on his target system and waits for a toner lock.

Enigma and Pulse can hear the emergency sound blaring in the cockpit.

Pulsa makes an assumption and says, 'He's not in front. He's behind us.'

Enigma makes an evasive maneuver after saying, 'I'm going to break hard left. Hold on.'

The jet instantly yanks to the left with the after burners glowing. Buzz Saw goes after them turning on his after burners and breaks left.

Enigma shouts for an update and asks, 'Where is he, Pulsa?'

Pulsa twists head behind as he says, 'He's hot on our tail. Let's shake and bake.'

Changing direction, Enigma yanks the joystick and flips the jet to the right. Buzz Saw continues on their tail.

Buzz Saw quickly regains his mental composure and gets back on track.

He creates another toner and locks on once more, and they get.

Frustrated, Enigma removes his breathing mask.

Pulsa does the same and says, 'Great. We just got beat by a fossil.'

Buzz Saw does not show any pleasure as he says, 'Get back to base for debriefing.'

It only took him a minute and a half to shoot them down.

Razor and Delta take off soon after Enigma flies back. They are confident they will be better.

Buzz Saw watched them taking off and give them time to get in the air and settle.

Delta wants to get this over with and says, 'I will set a time from when the exercise starts. It is only three minutes. We evade him for three minutes, we win.'

Razor thinks the same and says, 'Don't worry. We are good to trot. Bring it on.'

Buzz Saw flies by the side of them and says, 'Gentlemen. Are you ready for your lesson in high manoeuvre? We will begin in now.'

Razor breaks hard right and goes supersonic and says, 'He's going to have to catch us. Have you put the clock watch on?'

Delta checks the timer and says, 'We have two and a half minutes left. Make every second count.'

Buzz Saw is hot on their tail, flying a few feet below them on an angle. He wonders what his next move will be while biding his time to shoot them down. He wants to see how Razor skills are. They change course, banking left, but nothing shakes off Buzz Saw.

Delta checks how much time is left and says, 'We only have a minute left. keep it up.'

Razor can see him behind them from the curvature they are flying at and says, 'We've got this. He hasn't enough time to get a lock on us.'

There are only thirty seconds left for Buzz Saw to get a tone on them. He switches on his target system to begin a lock. Only twenty seconds left to get a toner on them. The jets are now weaving from side to side interchangeably for Razor to avert getting a lock on their jet.

Buzz Saw is still able to get a lock and they are metaphorically dead, inside the three minutes with three seconds remaining.

Delta snaps his breathing mask off in frustration and says, 'He got us with a five second window. Man, he's good for a dinosaur.'

After having two more dog fights with Venom and Trojan and Lobster and Fox, it is only Cougar and Storm left to get inside three minutes.

Cougar has been making checks on her equipment inside the cockpit while waiting for their turn. She is calm and collective not thinking about the training exercise. She seems to be distracted from work as her comms squawks.

Storm notices her mind is elsewhere and says, 'Cougar. Its us now. He wants us up in the air.'

Cougar snaps out of it and says, 'Yep. I got it. We have to beat Razor and Delta time of two minutes and fifty-five minutes.'

She moves the jet along to reach the runway. Then turns on the after-burners before taxiing along the tarmac and in seconds reaches fifteen miles an hour to take off and zoom up into the sky.

Cougar wants an update and asks, 'Can you see him on radar?'

Storm has no news and says, 'No. But he is around.'

Cougar tells him to use his peripheral view and asks, 'Can you see anything?'

Storm cannot see him above them or to the side and says, 'Nothing. Which means he must be below us.'

Cougar decides to make a circular pattern and says, 'Still nothing yet.'

Buzz Saw comes on the radio and says, 'So, you are my last student of the day. If you're like the others, this will be easy.'

Cougar gives as good as him and says, 'You're not dealing with an amateur. You are dealing with the best.'

Buzz Saw chortles and says, 'So, you're not too confident.'

Cougar is comfortable in her own skin and says, 'Bring it on.'

Storm catches him on the radar and says, 'Dead ahead.'

Cougar shows off by rolling the jet over their mentor leaving a few feet apart and stares at Buzz Saw upside down and then continues to roll to the other side of him.

Buzz Saw is not impressed and says, 'I've heard you are a bit of a wild cat.'

Cougar smiles at him and says, 'It's not for being in my forties.'

Buzz Saw smiles and chuckles as he says, 'Right. We will begin now.'

Cougar smiles saying, 'Catch me if you can.'

Both go into a horizontal spin.

Storm wonders what is going on and asks, 'Any longer, I'm going to be sick. Is there something between you two?'

Cougar is too focused to respond as they continue a horizontal death roll with neither of them backing down.

Buzz Saw is seeing this as pushing her limits to see what her abilities are and says, 'I can do this all day, Cougar.'

Cougar uses this to waste the three minutes and says, 'It's your time, not mine.'

Buzz Saw knows she will not get herself out of this. He pulls away and slams on the brakes to get behind her and switches on the target system, watching the faded orange dot track her. Eventually, he gets a toner within the three minutes with a second to go.

Storm is angry and says, 'Great. We got shot down because my partner had an ego problem.'

Cougar knows she let her partner down and did not expect to behave like a person possessed.

Buzz Saw has had enough for the day and says, 'Get yourself back to base for evaluation.'

Cougar now feels disappointed and says, 'I promise on the day, I will get us home.'

When Cougar gets them back on the tarmac, she walks ahead of Storm, past the row of fighter jets on either side. Storm can see she has a problem and would like to know what is bothering her. She is in a mind of her own.

Buzz Saw walks away from his jet and sees Cougar going past his direction and he briskly walks after her. He makes her face him.

Cougar does not want to talk but says, 'I'm on my way to change.'

Buzz Saw ignores her and says, 'We have to work together. I didn't choose this assignment. I see your skills remind me of your father. Something I have not seen in a while.'

Cougar cannot keep eye contact while she says, 'I'm sorry. It will not happen again. Sir, can I go now?'

Buzz Saw does not dismiss her and says, 'Get it out of your system.'

Cougar huffs and says, 'You caused my father's death. I know it was ruled as an accident. Next time, I will act in the mannerism befitting of an aviator. Sir.'

Buzz Saw smiles at her behavior and says, 'Right. Get out of year and attend the briefing.'

Cougar almost loses her emotions and says, 'Yes, sir.'

He watches her continue marching off and acknowledges Storm as he passes him.

In the lecture room, Buzz Saw expresses concern and evaluates each person's performance.

Each fighter pilot's flight was digitally recorded to show their skills on a projector. Their diverse skills will compromise the mission based on how they fly. He believes that if they get to know each other socially, they will collaborate better. For him to persuade them to change their habit, his team needs to learn about each other outside of work.

Buzz Saw suggests them going to his house for a barbeque and beer. His theory is that by getting them intoxicated and relaxed, they'll open up and drop their guard.

Knowing who they will be flying with is crucial for those prepared to die for their nation. Additionally, create a connection.

Finally Coming To Terms

♥

Last night wasn't as bad as I thought it would be. I sensed my wife's presence beside me, accompanying me. I underestimated the size of *Station Fallon* since it only takes me a few minutes to walk from her place to my friend's house.

Pam owns a bungalow while my friend owns a house, leading to the assumption that he has a family and she is single.

It's strange that I haven't seen her before, especially when I've seen a few other faces a couple of times. I wonder if I'll run into her again. There's no interest on my part when it comes to her.

The following day, everyone is up and prepared for work or college. A few different conversations are happening concurrently.

It brings back memories of my family, but my daughters have moved on to their own lives and homes.

As usual, his wife prepared breakfast for us with eggs, bacon, and pancakes with syrup. I usually don't have lunch and wait until dinnertime.

His family has welcomed me as a part of their own by involving me in their lives and seeking my opinions on their decisions.

If my friend hadn't let me stay at his place, I don't know what I would have done.

The Davis family, consisting of Holden, Amber, Emma and Luke, are Caucasian.

Holden is sixty years old and stands at six feet six. His build is filled out but has a toned frame from regular runs and light weights.

He has a short back and sides haircut with brushed-back hair. The hair is mostly brunette, with some gray mixed in.

Despite working in the navy, he maintains a sympathetic personality and hasn't let the culture harden him. The navy's desire to change its image aligned with his strengths, resulting in a favorable outcome. So, he was able to work his way up in the ranks quickly. His children were free to decide what career they wanted to pursue because he was laid back.

He served his country for forty years after enlisting at twenty-one in the navy.

Amber is his wife and their children are over eighteen and attending college.

Amber is 5'8" and in her sixties. She is slim with an hour-glass figure.

She has wavy brown hair that falls to her shoulders, which she ties in a ponytail.

Her personality is bubbly and carefree. She maintains a daily routine and remains stress free.

For work she helps out at the navy social club keeps her occupied and doesn't require her to bring work home.

Emma was in her late teens and five feet eight inches tall. There is no waist on her thin frame.

She has straight, mousy brown hair that is cut in a bob, with the front part of her hair tucked behind her ear.

She possesses a curious mind and enjoys asking tough or uncomfortable questions.

Her current goal is to study law in college and pursue a career in the legal system, either as a lawyer or legal secretary.

Luke's height is five feet six inches, and he is a couple of years older than his sister. He's got a flat stomach and a filled-out physique.

His hair is short, thick, and light brown with a regular cut and medium length on the sides and back.

He's introspective and keeps to himself. He's introspective and keeps to himself.

Similar to his sister, he's in college pursuing engineering.

After breakfast, I assist with cleaning the table by putting the dishes in the dishwasher and wiping the table. While I finish cleaning up, I observe them preparing for their busy day.

Holden has something he remembers and says, 'Oh, almost forgot. I'm having some colleagues coming over tomorrow for a barbeque. If you feel it is too much for you, you don't have to be here. Just giving you a head up.'

I appreciate his advance warning and say, 'After last night, I think I'm ready to face the world. Staring at metal gym equipment and four walls is getting a little boring now. It would be nice to see who you work with.'

Holden wonders what I'm going to do today and asks, 'Will you be doing the same old thing?'

I consider doing something different today and say, 'I think I will go for a walk and head to the local cafe. Maybe read a book.'

Holden half laughs and says, 'You are living now. I think you are finally moving on. Without realizing it.'

I know I'm not there yet, not feeling the motion and say, 'I'm just bored with lifting weight now. Feel like a change of view. I still talk to my wife. Every day. She keeps me company when I exercise and when I went to the bar last night.'

Holden grins and remains silent. I watch him leave for work.

I'm showered, dressed and ready to go out after ten o'clock. Today feels different since I've been here for some reason, but I'm not sure why. I have lost the motivation to challenge myself with workouts and feel the need to be around people.

Today, I feel like buying grocery for tonight and cooking for his family. Splurge on something extravagant to break the monotony. I want to express my gratitude for allowing me to stay here for as long as I want. Considering lobster, caviar, costly wine and a luxurious dessert. I am willing to rent a private jet to locate a supermarket that sells it.

I also decide to give the coffee shop a go which I walked by every day on my way to the navy gym.

Staying at the *Naval Air Station Fallon* is similar to being at a holiday resort, since all amenities are on one large site. The local supermarket is a fifteen-minute walk, which is where I will buy provisions for dinner tonight.

The feeling of a tight-knit community where everyone knows each other is present.

From the grocery store I purchase four entire lobsters, iceberg lettuce, cucumber, tomato, and the most costly wine available in the store. They gave me a thirty-dollar bottle, which was the best they could do. Unfortunately, they lacked caviar and the best dessert available was caramel-filled apple pie.

Once I obtain what I desire, I head back home and store the groceries in the fridge. Since it's only 11:30, I can still make it to the coffee shop for lunch, and have a cappuccino, and some cake.

When I arrive at the coffee shop, I choose a window seat to enjoy my drink and carrot cake with frosting while observing people. As I relax, I superficially listen to other people's conversations without paying attention to the content.

Then I hear the door open. I am surprised to see the woman I met at the bar, and I struggle to remember her name. It is on the tip of my tongue. The name Sam and Cam come to mind but I feel it is neither her name. I watch her go up to the counter and place her order while I try to recall her name. It seems like she's too preoccupied with placing her order to notice me. I feel at ease when I stare at her. My eyes keep gravitating towards her and I don't know why. My guess is that I find her to be different and original.

When she goes to walk out with her order, she turns round in my direction and notices me as she's about to leave. I assume she will not remember me but she smiles as she sees me and comes over.

I feel nervous now having to make conversation with a stranger. The only time when I would talk to a woman was when I wanted their business. I had something to talk about. Now, it is talking about nothing to make conversation. It is something I have never had to do for forty years. I have no idea what to say to her.

Still struggling to remember her name and hope she doesn't ask me if I know.

She glances at my drink and cake as she says, 'Hi Ethan. I see you went for a cappuccino. Great minds think alike. I've nether seen you in here before. This is my second home.'

I struggle to know her name and say, 'Hi. It is my first time here. I always walked past it on the way to the gym. Wondered why I never saw you around.'

She takes a seat which I was not expecting and says, 'I wonder why I haven't seen you around Ethan.'

I tell her about the gym and say, 'I kept myself to myself. Are you working at the bar again tonight?'

She continues to smile and says, 'Yeah. Will you be coming again?'

I continue to think hard about her name as I say, 'Not tonight. I'm cooking for my hosts as a way of saying thanks.'

She almost worries and says, 'You going back soon?'

I see in her eyes she may want me to stick around and say, 'I'm not sure. I have got used to doing nothing. Not having to boss anyone around. But, I'll need to go back soon. Looking at a months time.'

She appears relieved and says, 'Well, I have to get going. I have to go back to work. Maybe I'll see you again.'

I blurt out without realizing when I say, 'I hope so. I mean, that would be nice. Maybe bump into each other tomorrow here.'

She gushes and not sure if she notices herself doing it and says, 'Maybe. I'm always here around this time.'

I glance at my watch to see the time and say, 'Of course, Have a nice rest of the day.'

She walks out and her cute bum keeps catching my eye. I realise what I'm doing and quickly stop.

It's nearly three o'clock by the time I return to the house.

I boil the lobsters and add flavor to the water with sliced lemon. As I let it boil, I chop up the iceberg lettuce, cucumber, and tomatoes for the salad.

I lay the table with fresh flowers after preparing salad in a bowl.

I put the apple pie and caramel in the oven, but it's not turned on yet. Before I relax, ensure that I haven't left anything out.

It's past five o'clock and I hear the daughter's footsteps first, followed by the son's footsteps twenty minutes later and so on.

Every newcomer is taken aback by the sight of the table set with open bottles of wine and a bucket of ice with chilled beer.

Everyone must be seated before I serve starters, and Holden is the last to arrive, after six o'clock. I used what was already in the fridge to prepare a meal.

Before asking Emma and Luke, I poured wine into the Holden and Amber glass. Then pour out for them.

I stun everyone with my glass cups filled with prawns, lettuce, dill sauce, and lemon juice.

I ask them to eat up.

Everyone savors the starter in silence, amazed by its incredible taste.

The next dish consists of lobsters that were boiled, cracked in half and grilled to perfection. I sprinkled a light amount of cheese and chilly flakes on top to melt.

Their faces light up, and it brings joy to me. Once more, silence fills the room as they can't believe how amazing the food tastes.

As I mention the apple pie is for dessert, they sigh and express how full they are. I serve it pre-sliced on plates with a generous serving of thick cream on the side.

Interestingly, they always manage to make room for dessert and, just like with the starter and main course, they express their enjoyment of the apple pie and cream.

Upon finishing their meal, everyone pats their belly, amazed by how much they ate and unable to eat another bite.

After that, I clear away the last plates and cutlery and load the dishwasher. I make coffee that's as authentic as what you'd get in a coffee shop. Months ago, I purchased an espresso machine mainly for myself. It heats up milk and produces a range of flavored coffees.

While sipping our hot drinks, I express my gratitude for their warm welcome and patience with my silence and distance. While sipping our hot drinks, I express my gratitude for their warm welcome and patience with my silence and distance.

I'm not sure what to talk about but say, 'I know I have been distant and keeping to myself. I needed that time to finally let go of the past. I will never forget he and it doesn't mean I will meet anyone.'

Amber never thought of me as a nuisance and says, 'You needed the space to grieve. This is too much. You didn't have to do this.'

Holden tastes the wine and says, 'Ethan, this wine is gorgeous. And I know it is not eight dollars.'

I try not to go embarrassed and say, 'One other thing. Holden, you have a great family. The kind I wish I still had with my family. Again, you gave me the space I needed, and this is my way of saying thank you.'

Holden thinks nothing of it and says, 'Any time. And there is no rush for you to leave. You can go home when you think it is the right time.'

Amber follows up with saying, 'There will always be a home for you here. You have helped with tidying up the house, acting a taxi for our kids. And organizing our anniversary and paying for it. That already showed me how grateful you were.'

I leave after coffee and go outside, leaving them both to have time to themselves while the kids do their own thing.

Sitting on the porch in the backyard, I have a second bottle of wine at my feet and continue to sip my glass. I feel at peace with my wife's passing, like my heart has finally accepted it.

I envision a future where I am alone and work is the only thing in my life. I won't be able to find the same love with someone else.

I'm almost ready to head home, but I want to stay one more month to make sure I'm fully prepared to return to work.

I've been in regular communication with my colleagues at work and they've reassured me that everything is fine and there's nothing to worry about.

Amber quietly walks out with a glass of wine, happy that it's finally Friday, as I'm lost in my thoughts. She takes a spare chair and pulls it next to me.

Amber wants to know what I do for a living and asks, 'Before you came here, what did you do for a living?'

I'm totally honest and say, 'I work for an insurance company. Which I set up.'

Amber ears perk up and say, 'So, is that why you could take half the year off?'

I explain the irony, saying, 'My employees made me leave. I had a break down during a board meeting. My appearance didn't help.'

Amber laughs at me and says, 'I would have fired you. So, when do you think you will go back?'

I have no idea and say, 'I think it will be at the end of the month. But, I don't know. Going back to an empty house does not enthrall me.'

Amber has grown to enjoy my company and says, 'There is no rush. And if someone comes into your life, don't dismiss it. It is okay to move on and find someone else.'

I cannot think about another person right now and say, 'I'll leave it for now. I don't have the frame of mind to want to be with someone else.'

We sit quietly for a little longer before retiring to bed.

Moving On

♥

Holden has invited people over to a barbeque after 5 pm today, which is Friday. In the meantime, he plans to marinate the meat and tidy up the house. As it's his forte, he desires the house to be vacant.

I brought a book with me and decided to head to the local cafe after midday. Hoping to see her again is a part of it. Her name escapes my memory.

I'm sipping my cappuccino by the window, trying to read, but I can't help but notice the couples outside saying goodbye with smiles and laughter. Although I wanted what they had, I wished my wife was here.

I take a quick look at my watch to figure out when I can return to the house.

If the time had passed, she would enter to have her coffee. If I've been too engrossed in my book, we might have missed each other. Or she left quickly to avoid bumping into me. I'm curious if she was just being polite when she said she'd see me around.

While turning the page and taking a sip of coffee, I'm delighted to see her again and wonder why I have butterflies in my stomach.

It seems like she's eager to keep company once more. With a smile, I offer her a chair and she seems enthusiastic to talk.

I can't recall her name and end up saying, 'How are you? It seems like last week I saw you. Even though it was only yesterday.'

She seems pleased to see me and says, 'Ethan, I have something to ask you. You mention you do insurance. Do you do life insurance?'

I'm taken aback, she remembered, and says, 'Yes. We do. All I will need is your full name, address and date of birth. And your bank account. There is a questionnaire to fill out health history and I can have it set up in twenty-four hours.'

I observe her relief and wait for her to jot down her details on the paper. I need to discover her name again and then wait patiently as she writes down the necessary details. Patiently, I stare at the paper, waiting for her to write her name. She places a piece of paper on the table and I watch her write her name. Pamela's name finally comes back to me. But I remember, she prefers Pam.

I thank her by her name when I say, 'Great Pam. That is all what I need. Can I also have your telephone to call you when I've arranged the insurance?'

Pam does not hesitate and says, 'You can call anytime. Or text. No problem. Would you like another coffee?'

I realize I finished my coffee and say, 'Yes. Thank you.'

Finally, I know her name and have her number. I use a note app on my cell phone to keep her details. I plan to set up her policy later.

Pam comes over with the drinks and takes a seat as she says, 'I'm so grateful for setting up the life policy.'

I think nothing of it and say, 'No problem, Pam. Thanks for the coffee. And the business.'

We change the conversation by asking about each other's family, backgrounds, and activities outside of work. She's still unaware that I work for myself as an actuary.

Pam has been ambiguous about her involvement in the Navy's paperwork and inventory management. For my personal interest, I'd like to know if it's armory or stationary.

I believe we're becoming good friends and appreciate her company. Pam's hand movements and facial gestures greatly enhance her communication when talking about her past.

Despite our different backgrounds, we still share similar morals and preferences.

I notice how cute she is wearing a fitted blouse and three quarter length beige chinos and say, 'I think it is contagious. A friend of mine is having one today.'

Pam laughs and says, 'I guess it is. You found your home then, the other night. You had a few.'

I recollect and hope I did not embarrassment myself as I say, 'Ah, yes. To be honest, I didn't think I would see you again. I'd never seen you before in the last five months I've been here. And now twice in one week.'

Pam explains herself, saying, 'I normally wouldn't come in here. But, somehow, I fancied doing something different. So, you're lucky or else you wouldn't have bumped into me.'

I notice a part of me is glad, but I hide it when I say, 'I never asked what you do when you're not serving drinks.'

Pam happily tells me as she says, 'I work in the navy.'

I find myself wanting to know more about her and ask, 'So, what kind of work do you do?'

Her work as a pilot does not define her, so she avoids talking about it. Her profession changes how people perceive her.

Pam does was reluctant to tell me and then says, 'I work in the clothes store selling uniforms.'

I thought her job would be more adventurous in her personality and ask, 'What is that like? Only seeing people you work with and trying to sell the latest work clothes?'

Pam finds my sense of humor funny and says, 'Yeah, I never thought of it like that. It can be boring seeing the same color beige and white clothes.'

I think she wants something more out of life and says, 'Don't you want something more exciting out of life? Not that what you do is not exciting. You appear to seek adventure.'

Pam is intrigued by my perception and says, 'Maybe I want to take the high sea. How do you find working in insurance? Interesting? You look the type to want to run your own business. Rather than work for someone.'

I find her perception impressive and say, 'Maybe I want to know what it is like to own my own business.'

The conversation is so engaging that we both forget about our commitments. Before going to her event, Pam wants to stop at home first.

It's amusing that we both have barbeques to go to. Pam joked that I can call her and join her party if I didn't enjoy mine. We both express the same sentiment and depart, hoping to meet again before I leave.

Once again, I find myself gazing at her as she leaves first, before I clear away our cups.

It would have been great if we could have stayed here until closing time. Pam was refreshing and helped me forget about my loneliness. Pam made me realize I don't want to be alone anymore, but I'm not interested in a new relationship. My wife is my one and only soul mate, and the only person I want to spend the rest of my life with. My wife is my one and only soul mate, and the only person I wanted to spend the rest of my life with. My heart belongs to only to her.

I dread the thought of returning to a vacant mansion. I wish I could spend more time here with Holden and his family for their company. Also, meeting up with Pam for coffee.

Pam is amazed that she has met someone who can stimulate her thoughts for the first time. Instead of going to her boss's house, she preferred spending the rest of the day with Ethan. She regrets not asking him to join her barbecue for company.

Ethan's scraggly beard and wild hair make him cute in her eyes. She thinks Ethan resembles a caveman and wonders if he has a hidden club.

Although he's not her type, his thoughtful nature shines through when he's asked serious questions.

She hates it when a man tries to be funny or impress her, but he didn't do any of that. She prefers men who are open, honest, and show their true personality. Pam desires a man who isn't afraid to show vulnerability, not a boy.

Pam is unable to wipe the smile off her face as she walks home, still thinking about him before heading to the barbeque.

As I make my way back to the house, my mind fixates on Pam and how at ease she is with herself. She seemed very mature, and I didn't feel like I was talking to a child. She was capable of having a conversation independently and asking sensible questions. Fashion, celebrity gossip, and favorite TV shows are not topics I can converse about. The focus has to be on them and the people in their lives.

Pam has been cleaning the house as she waits for the barbeque. Before walking to Buzz Saw's house, her uniforms were cleaned, dried, and ironed.

When Pam approaches the house, she notices faint white smoke emanating from the backyard. In addition, she can perceive the aroma of the meat being cooked and faint, unclear conversations can be heard.

Hoping to be heard over the noise, she walks up to the front door and rings the doorbell. When she opens the door, she discovers it's her husband's wife. His wife greets Pam and escorts her to the back. Standing around Buzz Saw, cooking food on a gas barbeque grill, she sees Razor, Storm, Delta, Trojan, Venom, Enigma, Pulsa, Lobster, and Fox.

Upon seeing her colleagues' training with her, they realize she has finally arrived and greet her. They refer to one another by their call sign.

Buzz Saw wants a relax atmosphere and says, 'You're at my place. So, we go by our own names. We are not at work. So call me by my name.'

The ten of them, in unison, respond to his request and communicate by their actual names.

As they banter with each other, Pam laughs and the corner of her eye spots a familiar face and her draw drops as she recognizes someone she met recently. She thinks it is an imagination as she makes a double take.

I come out with a few vegetable and chicken skewers on a plate for Holden to add to the grill. As I pass him the plate, I notice his colleagues for the first time. All I know is Holden has brought home colleagues who he is their superior.

As I observe his colleagues, I'm shocked to see Pam here. I wonder how she knows Holden, as he is an admiral and she works in inventory.

Pam has the same confused expression on her face and we froze. Not sure how to approach each other. Not sure if to acknowledge we already know each other or pretend we have met for the first time.

Both of us smile out of politeness, and I wait for Holden to introduce me to them.

The first thing Holden does is introduce his colleagues as naval aviators. He names them by both their first names and call signs.

Their real names instead of their call signs were Ethan as Hank instead of Trojan, Bob instead of Lobster, Steve instead of Razor, Colin instead of Venom, Justin instead of Delta, Martin instead of Enigma, Simon instead of Pulsa, Roger instead of Fox, Bud instead of Storm and Pamela instead of Cougar.

I soon realize why Pam was called Cougar at the bar and she does not work in inventory.

Pam goes embarrassed, not knowing where to stare. I now know she is actually an aviator. Before I can be hypocritical and judge her, I'm introduced, and the truth comes out about me.

Holden continues watching the heat of the grill as he says, 'Guys, this is an old friend I've known since finishing high school. When we finished college and I joined the navy, he decided to get a sensible job. But, it paid off as you are standing in front of a multi millionaire. He owns his own insurance company.'

While the other guys are conversing with each other and jesting, Pam and I stare at each other, wondering why this feels awkward when we are only friends.

As we stand there frozen, waiting for the other to react, Amber and the kids come out, who distract us from being awkward around each other.

Before our stand off gets anymore awkward, Amber gets her attention and asks her to hang out together while the boys enjoy their themselves. Amber pulls Pam's hand to persuade her to spend time together. Pam walks with her while still being transfixed on me.

As I'm conversing with her fellow pilots, I cannot help glance over at Pam talking to Amber. I pretend to be listening and understanding what they are talking about while focusing on her.

Paranoid, she is criticizing me for misleading her to think I was a regular joe insurance salesman. Not sure if I've lost her as a friend.

Even though it concerns me, I'm only here for another three weeks and so it will not matter if our friendship ends.

Almost eleven o'clock now and the barbeque has finished and all the food has been eaten. Holden pilots have left acceptance for Pam.

She is sitting on the wooden steps of the porch, staring into space with a glass of wine. I can see she is a little cold and find myself gravitating towards her and find a blanket to put gently around her back. I sit next to as I finish wrapping it around her.

Pam smiles, showing her appreciation, and finds her leaning on me. It spooks me, as I expected her to push me away.

I've not felt another person on me in a long while.

Amber was about to walk out on to the porch when she sees Ethan with Pam and gently smiles with a twinkle in her eye and stands by the door feeling happy for him.

She cannot help wonder if they would make a wonderful couple as they sit on the steps keeping each other company.

Holden goes towards the back door see Amber observing his best friend and his aviator.

He holds his wife in his arms and finds her cute, doting on them. Then he motions her to leave them alone and slowly walk inside.

We have been huddling each other for a moment as I wonder how to spark a conversation. Whether to discuss the elephant in the room or pretend earlier never happened. As I go to say something, Pam speaks first.

Pam calls out the obvious and says, 'I didn't want you to know what I did for a living. I thought if I told you, you would not get to know me. I assume you did the same.'

I almost laugh before I say, 'I didn't want you to be fascinated by me being a millionaire. I wanted you to see me.'

Pam goes to laugh as she says, 'I still can't see you for who you are with all that hair and beard.'

I laugh at her humor and say, 'What if I shaved and cut all my hair off to where it used to be?'

Pam gently knocks her shoulder into mine and says, 'I would like that.'

I think of earlier and say, 'I don't know about you, but I felt like you hated me for deceiving you maliciously. When, for the reason already said, would be overlooked.'

Pam thinks the same and says, 'I thought the same. I assumed you hated me for lying to you about my job. I made a new friend to soon have it taken away.'

I want to get to know her more than a friend and say, 'Maybe we could meet in the coffee shop at the time you go in.'

Pam smiles and says, 'I would like that. Until you leave town.'

Even though I do not know Pam and we have only begun a friendship, I feel there is a bond forming as I feel her body against mine and smell her hair. We spend sometime not saying anything in comfortable silence.

Pam finds it strange how a man who has not taken care of himself can smell so nice with an expensive fragrance and his clothes smell so fresh. She finds him sweet and wonders how she had never met him until now with a small community on base.

She wants Ethan to walk her home to her actual home and realizes she put her true address down on paper and he hadn't noticed.

I check my watch and realize how late it is and say, 'It is close to midnight. I think your boss and his family are already in bed. There are no lights on.'

Pam glances behind her to see for herself and says, 'I guess I better get going. Even though the station is secure, I still get scared walking by myself.'

I'm glad she asked and say, 'Sure. I'll walk you home. I'll most likely scare them away with the way I look.'

Pam laughs again as we get up and walk to her place.

When we arrive at her place, I forget this house was not the house I originally walked her two nights ago. Where it is Saturday tomorrow, I wonder if to ask her if she is around to meet up.

I cannot help enjoy her company and want to spend more time with her. While I get myself in a knot about asking her out as a friend, Amber takes the weight off my shoulder by suggesting it herself.

Pam fiddles with her door key while standing in front of me and shyly asks, 'Do you want to meet up at the coffee shop tomorrow? Or tomorrow night.'

After I feel a warm joy in my heart, I do not hesitate to say yes and we agree a time before she goes inside. Upon feeling a warm joy in my heart, I readily agree and we schedule a time before she goes inside.

Letting Go

♥

Over coffee, Pam and I enjoy each other's company and never run out of things to talk about. I find it enjoyable to see her smile and her nose crinkle.

Pam finds herself admiring Ethan even more and is less bothered by his looks. She is curious about how he would appear without the wiry afro hair and overgrown facial hair.

The mechanism of flying a fighter jet has caught my interest, as I wonder why the wings have to be open during takeoff.

Pam is in her element and says, 'Well, to increase the lift at low speed. You only need fifteen miles an hour to take off. If the wings are closed, less wind can get under the wings. What does an actuary actual do?'

I try to explain as interesting as possible as I say, 'Well, it is measuring and risk of future events. So, we have to calculate the what the cost would be if it happened. Then, the insurance cost is driven by the chances of the event happening. There are not a lot of insurance companies which insure large assets. So, that is where we come in.'

Pam leans forward on her elbow being fascinated, and asks, 'For a fighter pilot, how would you measure the probability of crashing a fighter jet?'

I realize there is so much she does not know and says, 'Holden helped me to actually secure a contract to insure your planes. I had to look at how many planes you guys have crashed. Then compare to how far apart they happened over the years. Plus factoring in the training involved so you pilot prevent crashing them.'

Pam thinks she is worth it and smiles as she says, 'Did I not tell you I'm the best?'

I almost laugh as I find her response humorous and say, 'It could have helped save the navy some money. Is that all you'll be good at?'

Pam leans forward as she continues smiling and says, 'That's not the only thing I'm best at.'

I'm beginning to find her cute and unexpectantly finding her attractive and say, 'I wonder what they are.'

Our gazes meet, and we're oblivious to the amount of time that passes. As our noses nearly touch, my mind begins to imagine what kissing her would be like.

Pam doesn't seem to realize how much we've invaded each other's personal space. She seems relatively comfortable.

After a moment, Pam realizes she is eyeing me up and awkwardly pulls away while adjusting her posture. She seems to intentionally avoid eye contact with me.

I react by staring my coffee as a focal point to help Pam feel less embarrassed.

There is now awkward silence, and we hastily create small talk. We're shifting our focus to relationships.

Pam has a personal question and asks, 'Do you have someone at home waiting for you?'

I almost hide my past, but she deserves the truth and says, 'There was someone. We were married.'

Pam quickly says, 'I'm sorry. Was it amicable?'

I wish it was the case and say, 'She passed away. It's okay, it happened a while back.'

Pam quickly touches my hand and says, 'I didn't mean to stir up feelings. How long ago, if you don't mind me asking?'

I'm okay with it and brush off her guilt as I say, 'You don't have to feel awkward. You weren't to know. And no, I don't mind. It will sound stupid. My wife died five and a half years ago. I spent five years avoiding grief. Was eventually forced out of my own company to begin grieving. I was never like this. I wore two thousand dollar double-breasted suits. Sharp crisp shirts and fancy corporate ties. Was clean shaven and had no hair.'

Pam is curious about who she was and says, 'It is not stupid. No one has the right to tell you how long you should take to grieve. What was she like?'

I picture my wife before I say, 'Her name was Trudy. She was the same age as me. A great mother and a best friend. I assumed we would grow old together and be grandparents together. But life took that away. She gave me three daughters before passing away. They work for the company and are helping to run it while I'm away. I came here to grieve properly for my wife. I let work try to make me move on. Instead, I ended up looking like this.'

Pam laughs at me as she squeezes my hand and says, 'I didn't want to say, but now you brought it up. Ah ah ah.'

I laugh with her and eventually go to ask, 'And you? Not seen you with a husband or boyfriend.'

Pam goes quiet and stares into the coffee before she says, 'Never had the opportunity. Put my career first. As I excelled, it put a lot of guys off. Being in a profile role.'

I understand where she is coming from and say, 'I can't imagine someone from inventory asking you out for a date.'

Pam exaggerates a laugh and says, 'Ah ah ah. You're really funny.'

I go serious and ask, 'Is there anyone you like? You plan on asking out?'

Pam folds her arms on the table and leans forward as she says, 'No. So, hangout together until you head home.'

I'm feeling glad she asked and says, 'Sure. We can keep each other company. What do you fancy doing over the next four weeks?'

Pam thinks small and says, 'Coming here is good enough. Meet for coffee every lunch time.'

I think bigger and say, 'We can always spend time away from here. On the weekend. And find some nice places to eat during the week. You're forgetting I'm a millionaire. Don't let the beard fool you.'

Pam laughs again and says, 'Well, I'll leave it to you to choose the places. I don't exactly have any ideas outside this coffee shop. Less much the station.'

I watch her cute sad face and say, 'I'll do some searching online and organize our first outing. You won't have to worry about money. I'll cover it.'

Pam goes nervous as she fidgets in the chair and says, 'I want to pay my way. I don't feel comfortable you paying my half. We are not dating or in a long-term relationship.'

I reassure her by saying, 'Yes, but it is me choosing the activity. It is not fair to ask you to pay half if my choice of event is extravagant. At the same time, you admitted to not knowing any nice places to go to around here.'

Pam doesn't understand and asks, 'What can possibly be extravagant around here?'

I require some time to ponder on what's nearby and inform Pam to wait until I come up with a plan. We need to go our separate ways and do our own things now. I pay for the coffee and clean up while she leaves to go back to work.

It is the weekend with three more weeks to go before I head home.

Once again, a week has flown by quickly. I have only three more weeks before I have to return to LA.

We've exchanged many texts about the differences in our lives and what we hope to achieve in the next ten years.

The laughter between us has been like nothing we've experienced before. We share the same dry wit, which makes our sense of humor very similar.

Waiting for Pam's reply to my message has made me feel anxious. My impatience grows if I don't receive her text response within five minutes.

From time to time, Pam sends me a text asking if I'm okay. If I don't respond within a specific time frame, she follows up to make sure everything is okay. I saw it as a sign of her caring for me, and it was cute and endearing.

During my activity planning, I reflected on my time here and did some soul-searching by staring in the mirror. I've noticed a significant change in my appearance from six months ago. I seem revitalized instead of drained and ragged. When I look in the mirror, I see happiness instead of sad.

Additionally, I explore my emotions and no longer feel weighed down. I no longer feel the dull pain.

Now, I want someone for company, and Pam is that person.

I'm on a tight schedule and need to be at Pam's house in 30 minutes. I haven't showered yet because I decided to cut my hair and beard. I'm thinking of cutting my hair now. I've been thinking about it for a while now, for the past few weeks.

I retrieve my hair clipper from my suitcase and give myself one last glance. I'm finally ready to let go of my past and see what the future holds.

With each stroke, I see clumps falling off, and I catch a glimpse of my former self. The more patches of hair I lose, the more I resemble my old self.

My hair cascades down my chest and back, tickling my neck and shoulder with each clump that falls away. The act of losing my matted hair, turning into dreadlocks, has been reinvigorating.

Watching my old self fall and seeing a clean shaven head is a moment of euphoria.

With nothing else left to shave clean, I turn my attention to my unruly beard. Loose hair gets into my mouth and it's hard to remove. I find it especially challenging when I have loose cuts on my fingers.

The amount of hair on the floor could create ten wigs. After finishing, I collect the scraps and dispose them in the kitchen bin.

There's nothing better than taking a shower right after getting a haircut. Observing the loose cuttings flow down the shower tray and drain.

I feel like I have a new lease on life, with a spring in my step. I feel as though I've been given a fresh start to savor all that life has to give.

For some reason, I wore the three-piece suit that I was going to wear when I returned. I don't know why I feel like wearing it after years, for my first time, going out into the world.

As I put on my suit and stare at myself in the mirror, I hear someone walk into the bedroom. I believed that the house was empty.

Amber stares me up and down as she smiles in admiration and says, 'Now, I see the real you. Now, you are ready to go home.'

I turn to her and stare back as I say, 'I never thought I would see myself shaving my hair off. This is the day I have moved on in the next chapter of my life.'

Amber jokes, saying, 'I don't think she will recognize her date.'

I correct her saying, 'This is not a date. She doesn't see me in that way and nor I. And I'm not into pilots. They have ego and are full of themselves. I just find her interesting as a person and someone for company. Before I head back.'

Amber thinks differently and says, 'For someone who doesn't fancy her, why the expensive suit? Thats got to be at least five hundred dollars.'

I find myself questioning my thoughts and say, 'Two thousand dollars. And, I want to feel good about myself. Catch up with what I have been missing out on.'

Amber still sees it as a date and says, 'Where are you going?'

I know what she is going to think when I say. 'Las Vegas. Using my jet to fly us there. Not sure what we do from there. Need to get out of here.'

Amber thinks she has proven her point and says, 'We will have to agree to disagree. Make sure you don't hurt her. I like her.'

It's time to go now since I agreed to pick up Pam at eleven. We need to make it in time for our one o'clock lunch.

Pam has been practicing the attack run on the factory in a simulation of being attacked while following through the mission. Repeating the training exercise with different outcomes of resistance. Each practice making it more real and hard it will be to make it home. Buzz Saw's assertion that there's no coming back from this is becoming clearer to her.

She considers this lunch to be a perfect break from her rigorous training.

I used Holden's car to pick up Pam from her house. Upon arriving, I notice she's by the front door and wonder why she didn't wait for me to knock. I've never been inside her house and I wonder if she's embarrassed to show me around. It doesn't bother me either way.

With a smile, Pam walks over and gets in the car. Initially, she is surprised and thinks I am the wrong person to pick her up. As soon as she sees me, she's shocked by how different I look without my long, matted hair and thick, unkempt beard. To her, I'm like a completely new person.

My silver suit with a white shirt and corporate tie catches her attention, too.

As she climbs into the car, her face tells the whole story while she continues to scrutinize my appearance. The expensive suit and watch are making Pam realize my wealth.

Pam wonders where we are going and asks, 'So, what is the plan for today?'

I drive away wondering whether to tell her or let her see for herself and say, 'I'll show you.'

It seems like Pam is eagerly waiting for us to arrive.

I take us to the nearest airport from the naval base, which is a 12-minute drive to *Fallon Municipal Airport*, a small airstrip that only rents planes.

I arranged for my company's private plane to fly here and take us away.

Pam wants to know more about my business and says, 'You are more than just a millionaire. I think you're more close to a billionaire.'

I smile to myself and say, 'My company doesn't insure cars' house content. It insures military equipment such as tanks, ships as well as fighter jets. Also, luxury liners and billionaire homes. My company makes turnover in excess of over a billion a year. Profits of seven hundred million.'

Pam does not show any emotion, as if she is keeping her cards close to her chest and says, 'Well, I guess today is on you. Are you going to tell me where we are going? You have been really secretive.'

I decide to keep it a surprise and say, 'We will be going by plane. I own a private jet. Well, the company does. I have it on loan.'

As we reach the airport, I notice Pam's mind wandering, wondering what we'll do here. This location doesn't offer any provisions or entertainment. The only options available for rent are hangers and Cesena planes.

I slowly drive past the airplane hangers until I reach our plane, where the pilots are standing outside. As I drive nearer, Pam's mouth falls open in shock, wondering if it's for us. There are no other planes close by.

Together, we exit the car and I wait for her to approach me. To ensure they recognize me and guide us to the plane, I acknowledge who I am.

We still have a little while before departing, so I suggest Pam get comfortable and find out what she thinks about all this.

I struggle to decide how to tell her and say, 'I'm trying to tell you that this is who I am. This is not me trying to impress a friend. I didn't want to hide my real life.'

Pam laughs in shock and puts her head in her hands as she says, 'I still can't quite believe you are worth millions. You don't behave like you're rich. '

I do not know how to react and can only say, 'Yeah.'

Pam shakes her head and adjusts herself in the chair as she says, 'Wow. So, we're not going to Coffee Joe's then.'

I nervously smile and say, 'No. It's been years since I treated myself to a nice meal. I booked us a table for us to have lunch. Then thinking of a movie afterwards. Or maybe a tourist walk.'

Pam cannot stop laughing and says, 'Just like that. A private jet on stand by. Taking us where we want to go.'

I'm not sure how to react and say, 'This is not what I normally do. But it's been years since I treated myself.'

The pilot comes over to us to say, ' We are ready to take off now. Please put on your seat belts.'

Pam interrupts and says, 'I'll fly us. You organized our outing. It is the least I can do.'

The pilot appears bemused by her comment and says, 'Your guest is very funny.'

I stew over the idea as two pairs of eyes stare at me and eventually say, 'Paul, please can you find a hotel and I will cover the cost? Including all subsistence costs.'

The pilot takes off his hat and drops it on her head as he leaves the plane.

As we wait to be left alone, we can't stop grinning at each other.

After Pam places the hat on the table, she goes into the cockpit to prepare for takeoff.

As the engines start, I shut the airplane door and head back to my seat. I'm drumming my fingers on the table, pondering what to do alone.

Being flown by a friend feels weird.

Just when I thought I'd be bored by myself, Pam opens the cockpit door and motions for me to join her.

Pam waves her hand and says, 'Come and keep me company. It feels weird you being sat all the way back there. Take a seat next to me and keep me company.'

Watching her comfortably operate the instrument panel and switch buttons makes me see her differently. Her demeanor has transformed overnight, displaying a serious expression and pure concentration. The plane is guided by her towards the runway in preparation for takeoff.

We are moving slowly towards the tarmac. The tyres pick up every bump and gravel as the plane gently rocks. We're getting close to the edge of the runway.

Pam stares ahead, observing what is in front of us, and says, 'Fallon Municipal Tower. This is November Tango niner, zero, four two. Holding short of runway two. Requesting take off.'

A voice comes over the comms giving us permission to take off saying, 'Roger that. You clear for take off.'

Pam acknowledges the air traffic controller and says, 'Proceeding.'

The way she speaks in a soft tone and professionally makes it seem like she works for an airline.

I feel like a third wheel and ask, 'What do you want me to do?'

Pam has her pilot work mode and says, 'Just keep me company.'

As we taxi along the runway, I observe how she handles the plane. It's strange to watch how effortlessly she makes the plane jerk forward, accelerate and finally take off. I felt myself being pushed back into the seat.

Pam switches on the autopilot after we level off at forty-three thousand feet.

New Beginning

♥

I stay with Pam in the cockpit in case of an emergency. She has an idea and directs me to hold the control wheel on my side. Pam turns off the autopilot and I end up flying the plane myself.

I feel scared and nervous having our lives in my hands and say, 'Don't leave me now. Am I holding her steady?'

Pam is her self again outside of work and says, 'You're fine. I won't leave you alone. It's easy flying a plane. All you need to do is focus on two things. The *Direction Finder* to see we are flying straight and not turning. And the *Altitude Indicator* for height.'

I feel knots in my stomach from being nervous and say, 'Sure I won't crash this thing.'

Pam tries to be funny and says, 'You're insured, right? Now, the top row of switches and knobs are *Navigation Controls*. The two sticks side by side, in-between the two seats, are throttle levers. They are basically the accelerator, like in a car. The pedal on the floor is the break. After landing.'

I nervously smile and say, 'I think the insurance will be null avoid.'

Pam leans over to inspect the instrument panel. The aroma of her perfume and the feel of her soft skin against my chest overwhelm my senses. I take a deep breath of her scent and enjoy her sweet aroma. It's strange how seeing her as more than a friend affects me.

I wonder if she has flown other guys to impress to them and say, 'You must do this a lot.'

Pam has a confused expression and asks, 'How do you mean?'

I elaborate, saying, 'You must have flown a lot of men to impress them.'

Pam is puzzled and says, 'You're the first.'

I chortle at the notion and say, 'Come on. I must be your hundred man to fly for.'

Pam has a blank expression when she says, 'I've never taken a guy out on a plane. Except for my WSO.'

I show a confused face when I ask, 'What is a WSO?'

Pam smiles as she says, 'A weapons system officer.'

I still have no idea and ask, 'And what is that when it's at home?'

Pam tells me in layman terms, saying, 'Looks out for me with radar and handles the weapon system.'

Pam is amazed by how different Ethan looks without his hair and beard, and is captivated by his fragrance. She thinks that she's beginning to have feelings for him.

I watch her getting out of the seat and ask, 'Where are you going? You're not going to leave me on my own?'

Pam laughs and says, 'I trust you, Ethan. I saw champagne back in the cabin. Fancy some?'

I cannot believe she is leaving me unattended and say, 'Don't take too long.'

I feel weird drinking while flying. Since no one will believe I flew my own jet for the day, I'll take a selfie. Due to the risk of putting us in danger, Pam only has one glass as she will be flying us back.

Pam wants to ask me some personal questions and asks, 'How rich are you?'

I'm honest with no vagueness and say, 'About a hundred million. Tied up in assets, bank accounts.'

Pam's eyes almost pop out and says, 'What was your wife like?'

I almost have the air sucked out of me when she asks, 'She was great. She worked in the navy in LA. Introduced by Holden.'

Pam wants to know why I'm still single, asking, 'Will you search for another relationship?'

I almost instantly reply by saying, 'If you asked me five months ago, no. Now, I'm going out with a friend for a meal. Never thought I would socialize. What is going on with you and Holden?'

Pam goes quiet at first and then says, 'He flew with my father. I blame him for his death.'

I wonder how she knows and ask, 'What happened exactly?'

Pam does not go into detail but says, 'Told he provided cover, took out a few bandits before getting shot down.'

I wonder why my friend is to blame and ask, 'What did he do wrong?'

Pam cannot give a reason but says, 'It was a move not taught to do. Was asked to go against protocol. By Holden.'

I play devil advocate and say, 'Did you ask if he had a choice? Could he have stuck to protocol?'

Pam shakes her head in dismay and says, 'It is still his fault.'

I do not argue with her and say, 'I'm not going to get between you two. It's between you and him.'

Pam stares at me differently as she says, 'You are not bad looking without the beard. What will you do when someone asks you out on a date?'

I'm not confident and say, 'I'm a little old for someone to show an interest. Why aren't you married?'

Pam shrugs her shoulders as she says, 'I'm not interested in being a cougar.'

I give her a compliment by saying, 'If I were someone else, I would go out with you.'

Pam goes shy as she says, 'That is a nice thing to say.'

I reassure her, by saying, 'I mean it. If I was not me, I would make a pass a at you. Show off with my flying.'

Pam laughs and says, 'I wish you were that person. You're self sufficient. Handsome and smell nice.'

I smile and laugh back as I say, 'I wish were right for each other. I don't like seeing you single. You have a lot to offer, Pamela.'

Pam becomes embarrassed and unintentionally kisses me on the cheek while hugging me. Her kiss on my cheek lingers, and I feel like she won't let go of me. Her hug feels natural as I briefly embrace her. Pam quickly moves away after realizing what she's doing.

Silence filled the air, and neither of us knew what to say.

I eventually speak and say, 'I think I need a top up. Great champagne.'

After pouring my third glass, Pam takes the bottle and suggests putting the controls on autopilot before taking over.

As she pushes the button, she tells me to release the steering wheel and our eyes meet. She's so close to me that our noses almost touch.

My inhibitions have been lowered by the champagne, and I find it impossible to ignore how attractive she is.

Pam is struggling to resist her attraction to him since he became ten times more attractive. Her only desire is to feel the softness of his lips and determine if he is a skilled kisser.

Their gaze is fixed on each other as they unintentionally kiss and hold each other tightly. Ethan can't help but press his lips firmly to hers and refuse to let go. Almost six years later, he realizes how much he has missed this feeling. It's been over a decade since Pam has felt this way about a man. For years, she has been focusing on her career and taking long tours, without being with a man.

Ethan and Pam continue to embrace each other, with Pam finding his lips both edible and soft. Due to their lack of previous chemistry, she didn't anticipate anything happening between them. They viewed each other as nothing more than friends.

Ethan wants the moment to last forever.

The instrument panel makes a noise, startling us and ruining the moment. Without realizing it, we find ourselves laughing and connecting.

Pam goes to switch the noise off as she says, 'I must have knocked one of the knobs on the center control panel.'

I thought I would be relieved and say, 'That's a shame. I was enjoying that.'

We're unsure how to act around each other now. My intentions were never to turn this into a date or see where the friendship would go.

I allow her to take back control of the plane and open up to her when I say, 'I didn't plan this. I'm a bit shocked.'

Pam thinks the same and says, 'I did not intend to make a pass at you. It just happened. What are you thoughts?'

I'm honest with her saying, 'I had no plans to see if something could happen between us. I do not believe in having a fling. I'm heading back to LA at end the end of this month.'

Pam thinks about her mission and says, 'Thats why I never met anyone. Especially with what I have to face at the end of the month.'

I did not understand what she meant and ask, 'How do you mean?'

Pam does not want to discuss her mission and instead says, 'I will be shipped off on another tour.'

I feel like there's more, but I don't press her.

After an hour and twenty minutes, we arrive in Las Vegas just before 12:30. We take a taxi to the restaurant I reserved on the strip.

We're having lunch at *The Venetian Resort* and I'll be drinking the wine on my own.

Although we arrived early, the restaurant can seat us now.

Pam is surprised by the place Ethan has brought her to and thinks it feels like a date rather than just two friends getting coffee. Her previous dates have been to a burger place or the nearby cafe.

The hotel impresses both of them, neither having been to Las Vegas before.

Marble pillars and a wide reception desk complement the fully carpeted lobby area. The restaurant is behind reception and have to walk around behind to reach the restaurant.

One of the center tables has been reserved with a bottle of red, white, and rose on ice and was ready for us. Assuming Pam was not going to fly us here.

I offered Pam a seat by pulling out a chair and pushing her in. Then we each take our a menu and perusal. The variety of dishes leaves us both mesmerized, wondering what to order.

I make her feel relax by saying, 'There is no limit. Order whatever you want. My company is paying for it. It can be a business lunch. I think I will go for caviar as a starter and maybe go for a fish dish, as I mean to start.'

Pam raises an eyebrow as she says, 'Wow, you're not kidding. I feel guilty being here as a friend. I think you should have taken a date.'

I wave my hand as I say, 'I don't need a date. Just your company. I was thinking of doing the gondola afterwards. Then maybe window shop. It would have been nice if you could drink. I was not expecting you to fly us.'

Pam is thinking the same and says, 'I got carried away with trying to impress a friend.'

I wonder if she has plans tomorrow and ask, 'Are you seeing anyone tomorrow? Working at the bar?'

Pam nods her head as she says, 'Nope. Apart from washing a week's worth of clothes.'

I feel relieved and say, 'Great. I will buy us spare clothes and find two hotel rooms next to each other. Now drink with me.'

Pam serves herself a glass of wine and starts a conversation about our families and past experiences. Sharing stories from our younger days makes us both laugh.

Without realizing it, almost three hours have passed while we finished our dessert and coffee. We planned to ride the gondola after settling the bill, then shop for clothes for tomorrow.

In order for Pam to board the moving gondola, I've positioned my foot inside the boat to steady it. Holding my hand, she provides me with added support.

As we ride, we naturally move towards each other and embrace. It makes me happy that Pam can unwind with me and have a drink. I don't feel like she's showing me around and we're on the same level.

Based on our conversations and her intelligence, I can envision myself with her. It's not her work that makes me like her. What makes me like her a lot is her soft nature and thoughtfulness.

Pam is savoring the atmosphere while enjoying the Greek artwork above us.

I recommend that we go shopping for clothes after the ride before we proceed with the rest of the weekend.

I find it tricky to decide where to shop since I have unlimited funds, but she is on a budget, and I prefer the upscale stores. I'm not sure if she'll take offense to me offering to pay for her clothes. While we decide where to shop, we stand by the Gondola ride, pondering the notion.

I have a suggestion and say, 'I was wondering if we could go to the shopping area near the *Cheese Factory Restaurant*.'

Pam knows exactly what type of clothes shops they are and says, 'Sure. Get your clothes first and then go and look for mine. As you know, I don't have that kind of money.'

I make the decision not to offer to buy her clothes, but if she seems somewhat interested in something, I mention it in passing.

When we go shopping for my clothes, she playfully suggests the most outrageous items for me to try on. I share her sense of humor and she captures photos of me on her phone wearing these indecent tops and bottoms. My suggestion was for her to wear similarly awful clothes in exchange. We both find ourselves laughing and accidentally brushing against each other's arms or hands. My offer to buy the clothes was meant to be humorous.

Later on, we become more serious and Pam takes over my wardrobe choices, suggesting a complete revamp. Metaphorically speaking, discard the old to move on from the past and begin again. Pam has a gentle way of suggesting I change my appearance to help with starting a new chapter.

First Date Since

♥

I now have a new set of clothes, including work clothes, after an hour of experimenting. Pam insists that I wear my new clothes right now instead of waiting until later.

It's strange to wear my new clothes and realize their symbolism sinking in. However, I still have my wedding ring on, which I cannot take off.

Pam never assumed anything and gave me the space to talk about it.

We walk over to the cashier and join the queue.

I'm glad I met her as she has helped me to move on and ask, 'How do I thank you for helping to choose my outfits?'

Pam shrugs off my appreciation as she says, 'It was nothing. I had fun having an insight into how the other half shop.'

I use this moment to suggest buying her something and ask, 'What if you actually experience firsthand what it is like to shop like the other half?'

Pam chortles and brushes her elbow against my arm as says, 'Yeah right. That is not me. I'm happy wearing the clothes I can afford.'

When it's our turn to pay for the clothes and the register displays the total cost, I observe her reaction. She attempts to conceal the shock on her face. Her expressions can be really cute and I try to hide my smile.

I really want to treat her to new clothes, ignoring her reaction as I say, 'Let's leave my new clothes here and find a dress for you. I want to go out for dinner tonight. I have a nice place to take you to. I mean us. I mean, I want to.'

Pam smiles, watching me getting flustered and says, 'I get it. If you don't want me looking out of place, then help me choose a suitable dress.'

We couldn't stop looking into each other's eyes while searching for a dress in the women's section. It's a comfortable feeling. A woman approaches us and asks if we require assistance.

Pam informs the saleswoman that she is looking for an evening dress. With a smile, she surveys her multiple wardrobe choices.

While I stand around aimlessly, Pam accompanies the saleswoman and I browse some night dresses, imagining her wearing them. Shortly after, the saleswoman return with a clothes rail being wheeled over.

The saleswoman assumed we were a couple and requested Pam to try on the dresses for me to see.

A knee-length white dress with a yellow rose flower pattern was the first attire. The dress highlights her curves and she wears it well.

The second dress was a black one with a sheen, similar to the first.

Three additional dresses complement her skin tone and body shape. Pam had trouble deciding which dress was right for tonight because they all looked good.

Pam seeks my opinion and believes every dress is suitable for tonight. I stare at her face lighting up as she struggles to decide.

I stand there with my hands in my pockets and observe the dresses laid out across a cushioned bench.

Out of all of them, the one that caught my eye was a yellow silk dress, which is the dress Pam picks for this evening.

Once I chose the dress, I requested the saleswoman to help me find casual clothes for day wear. I don't let Pam opt out and wait for her to pick some items.

When we're finished shopping for Pam's clothes, I suggest paying for them instead of using her credit card.

Pam tries to get her head around how easy it is for me to pay and says, 'I feel like I'm taking advantage of your kindness and wealth.'

I reassure her saying, 'If I didn't want to, I wouldn't. And I'm not forgoing my own needs. You flew us here, so see it as your pay check.'

Pam soon comes round and her pride allows her to accept my gift.

Afterwards, we return to the hotel to unwind before dining out.

Once we reserve a room at *The Venetian Resort*, we flop onto the bed with our bags of clothes. The two-hour shopping spree has left us exhausted.

I'm going to take a shower to wear one of my new outfits. While Pam stays lying on the bed, we converse between the bathroom and bedroom.

I thank her for helping me choose my clothes and say, 'I had a great day. for the first time in five years, I have had fun.'

Pam laughs as she says, 'I'm glad you did. I cannot believe you bought some clothes for me. I will have to work two months to pay for them.'

I have no intention of accepting her money and say, 'It can be a treat for helping me pick out my outfits.'

Pam feels uncomfortable as she says, 'No. I cannot accept it.'

I walk back out of the bathroom as I say, 'You're flying us home. And, I can afford it. It's an hour's pay. Trust me, if you were rich, I would expect you to buy my clothes.'

Pam smiles and says, 'If I was rich, I would have bought you the shop.'

I laugh while I say, 'Yeah. I'll buy you the town tomorrow.'

Pam finds me humorous and says, 'I can't think of anything better to say.'

We continue talking while I was showering. I left the door open so we can hear ourselves talk.

Pam observes Ethan from her position on the bed while they keep talking. She's astonished by the muscular build of his upper body through the misty shower glass. Noticing his manly physique, her heart skipped a beat.

Suddenly, she catches his whole frontal nudity, giving her a full view of his middrift. She has a shocked expression, with her eyes nearly popping out of her head.

Ethan is completely unaware that Pam can see his whole body.

Her attraction towards him intensifies as she enjoys seeing his naked body.

Pam reflects on their time on the flight and imagines what he would be like in a relationship.

Once I'm done in the shower, I dry off and put on a bathrobe before stepping out of the bathroom. Allow Pam access to the bathroom.

I keep my robe on until it's time to change for dinner since we have some time. I get on the bed and wait for her to finish showering.

She feels comfortable around him, so she left the door open as well.

Their conversation continues while Pam soaks her body under the water flow.

Pam is wondering if he will catch a glimpse of her partially naked as she changes goes to wash her body.

I stare at the designer shopping bags and say, 'It is a weird feeling moving on. I don't have the dull pain anymore. Only the good memories.'

Pam talks over the noise of the shower, saying, 'You will never forget her. And you are going through the healing stage. You do know you can talk about your wife anytime.'

I appreciate her kind words and say, 'I appreciate it. I'm looking forward to dinner and having more drinks.'

The sound of the shower turning off makes her voice clearer to me. As I turn away from the bags, I unexpectedly catch a glimpse of her breast and the side of her nude body. I find the view appealing to the eyes. As I watched her dabbing her skin with the towel, I couldn't help but wonder what it would be like to date her.

I move closer to the bathroom entrance to improve our conversation while we talk. As I approach the entrance, Pam emerges and we nearly collide. We find it funny when we startle each other.

As soon as our eyes meet, we both stop and stare at each other. There is a warm silence between us.

We're touching each other's fingertips and unsure of what to do next.

Although no words are spoken or implied, we find ourselves walking towards the bed and clearing the bags off of it as if we go to lie on the bed.

We walk slowly to either side of the bed and meet in the middle as our mouths come together.

Initially, we kiss gently on the mouth by pecking softly on each other's lips. It comes naturally and doesn't feel awkward.

We hold hands and gaze into each other's eyes while lying next to each other. Gently, I brush the back of my fingers over her cheek. Closing her eyes, Pam feels my skin against hers and smiles while holding my hand to her face.

Next, I lean in and kiss her once more, resulting in a tight embrace where we passionately lock lips.

We were unaware of our chemistry, yet we found ourselves naked, with me on top of her and continuing to kiss.

I can sense her warm and soft bosom against my chest and feel the smoothness of her back.

Ethan's chest feels solid against Pam's stomach and his arms are strong around her. She's sexually attracted to his scent, and they continue kissing.

She soon senses his arousal as his erect phallus presses against her torso.

Her arms pull them closer than she suddenly desires him inside her.

After reading the signs, I position myself to enter inside her. I never thought I'd find someone who made me feel this way again, but it feels so natural.

Pam gasps as I enter her and her fingertips scrape my shoulder blades. I'm feeling a mix of emotions. I miss this feeling and desire to be with someone to experience it once more. I had a guilty feeling, as if I was betraying my late wife.

It feels amazing to be inside her and she smells wonderful at the same time.

I briefly contemplate extending my stay to spend more time with her and continue this enjoyable experience.

Pam climaxes in no time, and I can feel her muscles contract and grip my phallus. It won't be much longer until I release myself.

Both of us hold each other tightly and groan quietly from the ecstasy.

We lay beside each other, still in disbelief at what we had just done. It wasn't our intention to hope for intimacy with each other.

Pam acknowledges that she never expected mutual feelings to develop between us.

I observe her lost in contemplation, with her hand resting on her forehead, and question whether she is still in shock or remorseful about advancing our relationship.

She can't remember the last time she was intimate and can't believe this is happening. Her dangerous assignment briefly comes to mind. She wasn't bothered in her personal life at the time, since she never thought her life would change. Although he's here now, he won't be for long. Nevertheless, it made her question whether she would ever meet someone. Furthermore, she has a reason to avoid taking the flight.

She lies there, puzzled, contemplating her potential future.

I eventually asked her what she was thinking.

Pam hesitates to open up and then says, 'There is something I have to do. I was chosen because I have no husband to leave behind. And no kids. It did not bother me and understood the reason.'

I wonder what she is talking about and ask, 'What are you asked to do? And why does it matter if you are not married.?'

Pam stares up at the ceiling while she says, 'I have gone through life focusing on my career and never had an opportunity to meet someone. When I was hand picked for a mission, I had no one to think of. Now, I... this is going to sound stupid.'

I encourage her to tell me by saying, 'Go on. It won't sound silly.'

Pam places her hand under head as she continues to stare up at the ceiling and says, 'I know we have only just had something But, it is enough to have second thoughts on this job I have to do. And that is your fault.'

I somehow see where she is coming from and say, 'I get it. You have had a glimpse of what could be. When you were given the mission, your life was yesterday. Now, you have hope of finding someone. So, you want to have a chance of finding it I assume. When do you leave?'

Pam hides her sadness through her smile and says, 'In four weeks' time.'

I wonder how dangerous the task is and ask, 'What is the probability of making it back?'

Pam continues not to make eye contact as she says, 'It is a no return trip.'

It spooks me hearing her say she will not be around in four weeks' time.

I wonder how she is feeling and ask, 'What are you thinking with the idea of spending your last fourteen days here?'

Pam sighs and faces me as she says, 'When you join the navy, you know what you're signing up for. But to be told you will not make it home, it makes it different.'

I suggest an idea and say, 'You have four more weeks before you go away. I was planning on leaving in two weeks. How about I stay for an extra two weeks so we can keep each other company before you go? We can find something to distract you?'

Pam goes giddy and says, 'What do you have in mind?'

I have a few ideas and say, 'We can go away for nights over the next four weekends. Like, a mini holiday.'

Pam smiles and giggles at the idea and says, 'Does that include this? What we just did.'

I smile and feel like a kid again and say, 'Maybe?'

Pam wonders what the parameter is and asks, 'Is this a one off? Or the beginning of something while it lasts?'

I don't want a plutonic friendship with our remaining. time together and say, 'I would like more of this. Up till you have to go away.'

Pam is happy to hear that and says, 'So would I.'

We decide to skip dinner and stay in the hotel room. Instead, we choose to have sex a few more times.

The following day, we check out and make our way back to the airport to catch our flight home.

Before heading to the runway, Pam turns on her pilot head and performs some checks. As usual, she communicates with the control tower to obtain takeoff clearance.

As usual, I keep her company while watching her work the controls. She gives me occasional glances with a smile to show she is not ignoring me.

After takeoff, Pam wants me to pilot the plane again while she accompanies me. Being responsible for our lives again is making me nervous, especially since I'm not entirely sure what I'm doing. My lack of relaxation is apparent to her, and she finds it amusing.

Pam has an idea and asks, 'Do you want to do something crazy?'

I don't think I want to hear her idea and say, 'It depends on what you have in mind.'

Pam takes over and leads us even higher into the atmosphere without saying a word.

Temperature Rising

♥

As she ascends through the light blue sky above the clouds and heads towards the earth's surface, I can see the concentration in her face as she checks the controls. It seems like the sky is darkening as if it's turning into nighttime. As we approach space, I observe her struggling with the control wheel. The slight shaking of the plane might be due to thinner air during travel.

The lack of airflow to the turbines is causing a strain on the engines. The plane experiences vibration as a consequence.

Pam shows no sign of worry and says, 'This is the closest to heaven you'll ever be. We are riding along earth's surface before entering space.'

I stare out and see how bright the stars are above us and say, 'You can almost touch them. This is surreal traveling close to outta space. Is this okay?'

Pam continues to fight with the plane and says, 'We are safe. She wants to veer off and I'm keeping her on course. Just a minute longer.'

Nothing comes closer to heaven than this. I have a feeling my wife is near me, as I'm up this high in the air. I want to fully enjoy my time with Pam, so I'm avoiding letting my thoughts of my wife take over.

As I watch Pam confidently manage the stress on the plane, I find myself even more attracted to her.

Pam brings the plane to a safe altitude, and it returns to normal.

Upon our return to *Fallon Municipal Airport*, my pilots meet us there to fly the plane back to *Los Angeles*.

We've been staying in touch through text messages for a few days now. We've planned to meet again on Friday.

Pam has been sharing with me about the intensity of her week due to her secret training. She is keen on letting her hair down to switch off from work.

I thought a vacation would help her relax and I'm also long overdue for one.

I organize a trip without discussing with Pam to forget about life and have a carefree weekend.

The place we're going has some bars and sights to see, and it's a relaxing destination. Again, we will fly private. Considering the texts I've received from Pam this week, I'll ensure she takes a break from flying.

Our departure is scheduled for later today after she finishes work.

I choose to pass the time at the coffee shop with lunch while waiting for Pam to finish work and leave. My small holdall bag is already packed for the trip.

Pam and her team finished another training exercise and are now working as a team more efficiently. They simulated the mission by programming the fighter plane's flight system with similar terrain for their exercise.

The task required reaching the target within an four hours, hitting it in two minutes, and returning home before the enemy could attack.

Their instructor, Buzz Saw, has concentrated on the final leg of the journey, refining the accuracy of eliminating the SAMs and guaranteeing the plane and factory are demolished.

The task has been exhausting on both the body and mind, repeating it intensively. A stress-free weekend is needed by her and the other pilots.

As I wait in the coffee shop before surprising Pam, I reflect on my remaining time here. It won't be much longer before I have to leave for home. Only two more weeks here.

My two daughters have been trying to get hold of me. I've been avoiding them, not responding to their calls or messages.

I've gone through their messages a few times, reminding myself to reach out eventually.

I'm thinking about the weekend and imagining how it'll go. Wondering if our relationship will be intimate or platonic, I imagine what we'll be doing. The most important thing to me is having fun together, regardless of any outcomes.

The wait until six o'clock feels like an eternity, because that's when Pam will be free and we can leave.

To prevent the owner from asking me to leave, I am drinking my third cup of small latte.

I decided to stream a movie on my phone using the Wi-Fi to make the time pass by a little faster. I found a movie that lasts over two hours.

As the film nears the end, I realize it's almost six o'clock and gather my things to leave. The phone rings, and I see it's Pam, so I pick it up.

Pam sounds keen to get away as she says, 'It's Pam. This week has been a nightmare. It has been so stressful. I'm so forward to this weekend.

Can you be at mine in the next ten minutes and then wait to get out of here?'

I'm surprised how much she wants to go away and say, 'Sure. I'm at the coffee shop. It will take about ten minutes from here. We can get a taxi from yours to the airport.'

Pam goes quiet briefly and says, 'Oh. We are going out of town again. I thought we were just going a drive away. Anywhere interesting?'

I decide to keep it a surprise and say, 'You're not flying this time and so it will be a surprise.'

Pam sounds pleased on the phone and says, 'Well, what should I take?'

I think of the area we are going to and say, 'You can bring a bikini and a dress.'

Pam's voice goes excited and says, 'Great. I also just got paid, so I can pay for the drinks and food. You provide the jet and pilots.'

I almost laugh and say, 'Sure. There should be some nice restaurants to go to. Also, I want you to totally forget about work.'

Pam reaches her house as she says, 'Just got home. Will leave the door unlocked and so help yourself in.'

Upon entering, I hear her showering with the door shut, thus I wait in her living room.

My excitement about our trip is growing stronger, as we are only a few hours away from reaching our destination. I'm currently thinking more about how this weekend will go.

I'm hoping Pam is feeling the same level of excitement as I am for the breakaway to be enjoyable.

While taking a shower, Pam feels her stress melting away and looks forward to going away with Ethan. She wonders if Ethan would want to repeat what they did in Las Vegas. She wouldn't say no if the chance came up again.

She hoped he would bring up last weekend, but he never mentioned it. Pam refrained from bringing up the topic since he had recently moved on from his late wife. She didn't want to come across as insensitive.

With the possibility of intimacy arising again, she intended to pack her best underwear.

The topic of Las Vegas never arose in our conversation. I'm thinking about the possibility of having a repeat. I was hesitant to mention it while speaking with Pam, afraid she might have regretted it.

I heard Pam go to her bedroom to change after leaving the bathroom. She says something muffled through the wall.

I cannot cypher what she said and ask, 'What was that?'

Pam comes out of her bedroom with wet hair and says, 'I have been looking forward to this weekend since forever. This is what I need. To get away.'

I can see on her face how intense her week has been and say, 'This is exactly why I made an effort with this weekend. Just going to the bar or heading to Las Vegas again would not cut it.'

Pam wonders what I have planned and asks, 'Where are we heading? You mentioned about taking a bikini. Are we going to Los Angeles to the beach? Meeting your family?'

I smile, not being able to contain my excitement and say, 'Better. I promise you will not have any chance of thinking about work.'

Pam rolls her eyes, struggling to believe me as she says, 'With the week I have had. I think it will be a stretch. Not that I'm doubting you. I hope I don't ruin our time away.'

I feel for her as my life has no stress or worry and say, 'I have plans for going out for dinner and drinks. Also, going to the beach. So, I hope that will be a distraction.'

Pam smiles and sees me cute as she says, 'I know it will take my mind off. But, have doubts it won't. '

We hear the sound of the horn as the taxi arrives.

This time I have my pilot fly us to keep the weekend a surprise. Pam has no idea where I'm taking her.

Our destination is five hours and forty minutes away. Our arrival at the destination will be after 3:00 AM local time. There'll be a rental car waiting for us.

Sitting opposite each other on the plane, I watch her struggling to stay awake to keep me company. I let her struggle against fatigue until she can no longer keep her eyes open.

Resting her head to the side, she appears peaceful as she falls into a deep sleep. As I gaze out of the window, I'm glad that Pam feels so comfortable around me.

Pam has been asleep throughout the whole flight and startles awake when the wheels slam onto the runway with a bang.

Pam opens her eyes and dart forgetting she is on a plane with me. She rubs her eyes to stir awake and stares out of the plane to guess where we are.

After we can leave the plane, I carry our bags to the car and place them in the trunk. Then drive us to our accommodation.

Since it's still nighttime, Pam has no clue about our location and won't find out until daylight.

My adrenaline is pumping and I'm wide awake at only eight in the morning, all thanks to the thought of a potentially amazing weekend.

Our accommodation was more beautiful than I saw in the pictures on the internet. It over looks a beach a few steps away.

I decided to get us provisions for breakfast and mentally planned for the rest of the day. Tonight's plan includes dinner and a lot of drinking. Spend today relaxing on the beach and catching up on sleep.

I walked to the local market for pineapple, apples and grapes, while Pam stays behind and rests for my return.

I was caught off guard when I heard footsteps coming out of the bedroom as I was getting the fruit ready for the finger buffet. With an enthusiastic smile, I eat a piece of pineapple. Pam smiles back, relieved to not be in a work environment. She takes a piece of fruit for herself, biting on a grape as she observes me chopping up pineapple into pieces.

Pam smiles while chewing still and observes our surroundings before staring out of the back of the bi-folding doors, as she says 'Nice view. Something tells me we are not in America. Or are we in Miami?'

I casually take a view of the surrounding and say, 'Try Cuba. We are at a friend's place I made through an insurance deal. I said I would like to check it out before I consider buying it from him. It is situated next door to the beach. I have plans to take you out for dinner and then a bar for drinks..'

Pam continues smiling and says, 'You being here is enough for me. Happy to stay here all weekend and maybe you cook for me. We get a nice bottle of wine, a crate of beer or a bottle of bubbly in. Thinking a barbeque.'

I'm thrown off guard and ask, 'You're sure? I'm a great cook, but thought you would rather go out and sample Cuba.'

Pam compromises and say, 'Take me out to get food for tonight and maybe have a drink before we head back. I want a quiet night in. Just the two of us and no one else.'

I have visions of us having an intimate evening and say, 'Okay. We will need meat for the garden grill and plenty of alcohol.'

We both wore shorts and summer T-shirts to walk the streets of Havana.

While at the market, we become overly friendly and feel like we're on vacation as a couple. Pam and I walk from one stall to the other, looking for supplies, with her arms wrapped around mine. The discomfort is gone, and we understand our boundaries without communication.

We share the enjoyment of the culture, laughing and joking about our fondness for this place and how the locals seem serious, yet they naturally embrace tourists. Suggestions about what will go with our meal are given by the sellers. As I ask for advice on marinating the meat and the best seasoning, Pam observes me interacting with them. She's surprised by how polite and at-home I am.

I can't help but notice the way she stares at me, but I pretend not to notice. We don't need much time to gather everything before we head back.

We stumble upon a peaceful hut with tables outside on our way back to the beach house, where we can enjoy a quiet drink together. While

I choose a table and rest the bags of supplies on the ground, Pam goes to get the drinks.

As she walks towards the bar, I cannot help but admire her swaying behind. Briefly glancing at me, she senses what I'm doing.

We're enjoying the cold beer and each other's company in comfortable silence as the hot weather fills the clear blue sky, and the sun beats down on the ground. I'm starting to sweat as I feel a droplet roll down my neck.

We're glad we're here, smiling about this moment instead of being back in *Fallon*.. Savoring the sensation of frigid, flavored beer streaming down our throats, satisfying our thirst. As time passes, I find myself admiring her even more, and I can't help but wonder if anything might happen between us tonight.

Pam wonders if they will continue what they started in Las Vegas. The weather and atmosphere are influencing her to develop stronger feelings for him. She was eager to return home and spend some quality time together.

Considering the meat being exposed to the sun for too long, my recommendation is that we finish our beers quickly and return.

Can't Take Our Hands Off Each Other

♥

Pam attends to the wine bottle and pours us both a drink while I start the grill and get ready to cook.

When Pam goes to find glasses and a bottle opener, she decides to change into more comfortable clothes. Suitable for the weather.

While waiting for the heat to reach the correct temperature, I prepare the tomatoes and salad for the meal. My top got stained by a jet of juice, so I decided to remove it to prevent it from getting on my skin. Additionally, my top is pretty wet from walking in the sun.

As Pam turns from the kitchen counter with glasses of wine, she glimpses Ethan's chest and pauses. She can barely believe how solid his chest is and almost drops the glasses. He wasn't as noticeable in the steamy shower in Las Vegas. It increases her attraction towards him.

I sense that the grill is ready for the meat, so I place the steak cuts and apply the recommended sauce. I hear Pam walking over and turn to notice she is wearing only a two-piece bikini and cannot believe how curvy she is and her dark olive skin. I find it difficult to avoid staring at her in a sexual manner.

She has a toned body that her clothes fail to accentuate. She walks by me and places the wine glasses on the table, and I notice her cheeks peeking out from her bottoms.

As I look at her, I notice my body perspiring faster. I can see the appreciation in her eyes as she looks at my torso.

It's difficult for me to concentrate on not burning the food with Pam in her white two-piece bikini, watching over my shoulder, waiting for the steaks to be ready. Imagining our future together is making my feelings for her grow stronger. I imagined introducing her to my children and meeting her family. Wondering the possibility of either her moving to Los Angeles or me staying here and both of us managing how work will fit in.

However, I recall her task, which may result in her never returning.

Pam is on a kamikaze mission but wishes she wasn't chosen because of her feelings for Ethan. She's questioning if he's the one capable of providing her with love and a caring partnership. It's been years since she met someone who could be a suitable partner, and this is the first chance. She would prefer to get married, but any kind of relationship would suffice.

When she hovers over his shoulder to see how dinner is going, she cannot resist brushing herself against his back. She feels the urge to wrap her arms around him, but her rational side cautions her not to mess up the moment.

The dinner is ready to be served now, so take the seasoned steaks off the grill and put them on our plates. As we take a seat, we see that salad and a bottle of wine are already on the table. I observed Pam serving the salad on our plates, noticing her smile as she caught me looking at her. Initially, we eat silently, relishing the ambiance and surroundings.

I'm comfortable with the quietness, but I don't know what to say. It looks like Pam is savoring the meal and content with the silence.

Pam takes the dishes to the kitchen while I pour wine into two glasses and take them to two sun loungers near a fire pit. Shortly after, Pam emerges and we both take a seat next to each other on the upright loungers. We unwind as we watch the sunset on the horizon. I am gradually becoming tipsy and my inhibitions are starting to fade.

I wonder if she liked the meal I made and ask, 'How did you find the steak?'

Pam appears slightly drowsy herself and after she twists her body facing me, she says, 'It could have done with a bit more salt. Ah ah. Only kidding. It was nice.'

I gaze at the full body wine in my glass and say, 'Could have cooked a bit longer. But they tasted nice. Has this helped you to forget about work?'

Pam smiles and says, 'Work? This is the best distraction. if you don't mind, how rich are you?'

I remain silent to think..

Pam feels like she has over stepped the mark and says, 'I'm sorry. That is too personal. Ignore me.'

I wave my hand to indicate I'm not bothered and say, 'Do you mean the company or personally?'

Pam is not sure and says, 'Personally.'

I raise my eye browse having think and then say, 'In the bank? The last time I checked, I had about twenty million. In various accounts. My life style is basic. Don't live like a rich man. More of a hoarder. My daughters think I'm tight with money.'

Pam gulps her wine down and says, 'I need a top up. You? That wine was good. I'll open another.'

I agree with her and say, 'That was good. Only sixty dollars. The next one should taste nicer.'

Pam stumbles and turns round to see if I noticed and says, 'Wow. I thought it tasted of sixty dollars. I think I'm drunk.'

After stoking the fire pit, I add an extra log, stumbling in the process.

Pam is not long when she comes back and says, 'Top up?'

I steady her pouring arm as she fills my glass and says, 'Thats enough. Isn't this great? We still have tomorrow.'

Pam giggles when she almost over flows the wine glass and says, 'I want to stay here. I don't want to go back. Just you, me. And this great wine.'

I think the same and say, 'I wish we could stay here forever.'

Our chemistry intensifies as we stroke each other's arms while being close. I sense my own arousal and observe Pam's bikini top is revealing, and I can see she's feeling aroused.

We roll onto our sides to mirror each other's body and find ourselves looking into each other's eyes. No words are needed to acknowledge the intense attraction between us.

She briefly glances down and notices my strong attraction towards her, and her eyes show a pleasing expression. She touches my phallus to manipulate my emotions for her. Pam smiles as she teases and touches me, her eyes revealing how much she enjoys it.

My murmurs reveal my arousal as her curious hands explore through the fabric of my shorts. I widen my legs to inspire her to keep going.

As I massage one of Pam's breasts, I focus on her rock hard nipple, causing her to softly moan as I gently tweak and pull it. I watch her as she closes her eyes to intensify the experience.

We're both striving to make each other even more turned on. As we continue foreplay, we eventually begin to kiss passionately.

I played with her beautiful areola for a while and then moved my hands down to her vulva, using my index and middle finger to stimulate the folds of her labia. I rubbed the fabric of her bikini bottom against her folds, and she spread her legs to make it easier for me to reach further.

While we kiss, I sense her opening her mouth, savoring my actions of pleasing her. A few times, I flicker the tip of my tongue inside her mouth. Her tongue repeatedly touches mine.

Pam starts moving her hips to enhance the effect of my fingers on her delicate area. As I interpret her body language and vocal cues, I build up a momentum.

We can feel the dampness of each other's clothes due to my pre-cum and her lubrication.

I really want to take this further in doors and whisper softly as I say, 'It's getting cold. Let's go inside.'

Pam pecks at my lips as she says, 'Yes, it is. We'll go inside now.'

The fire is dwindling, so we're going inside with our drinks.

We both rise to our feet and she giggles as she notices my massive hard-on bulging through my trousers. I blush as we go inside.

Sipping on wine while lounging on the sofa, we talk about how amazing it would be to stay here and not worry about our obligations. Amused by the thought of doing nothing but relaxing.

While contemplating the notion, we gravitate towards each other once more and lean against one another. Our hands are lying close, almost touching, and my mind is filled with thoughts of making love to her. I sneak a peek at our hands touching and realize Pam is doing the same. We gaze into each other's eyes and our smiles fade.

We pick up where we left off, kissing and stroking each other.

The feeling of her lips brings me back to our Las Vegas trip.

Pam enjoyed the feel of Ethan's lips and wondered if they would eventually make love. She yearns for him to be inside her again since last weekend. She has missed their sexual intimacy.

It dawned on her that she had a crush on him since they met at her uncle's bar. She believed that running into Ethan at the coffee shop was meant to be. It became even more apparent when she discovered he was at her boss's barbeque..

Seeing him three times in a row felt too surreal to her.

The touch of her lips and bare skin against mine is arousing. I partially withdraw a couple of times to ensure her consciousness and awareness. Pam passionately kisses me while continually gazing into my eyes. As we explore our bodies with our hands, I feel the alcohol's effects fading away and my senses becoming more acute.

Pam motions for us to lie down on the floor and continue our encounter.

Pam reaches out her hand to take mine and then I get on top of her. I see her remove her bikini top and drop it beside her. She signals me to move her bikini bottom, making it clear she wants to take things further. Pam watches my reaction to her being naked and helps me take off my shorts.

Apart from my wife, Pam is the only other woman I've been with. As my feelings for her intensify, I'm experiencing a strange yet pleasant sensation.

Pam seems to know what I'm thinking and says, 'It's okay. I've got you. Make love to me.'

I feel my heart racing as I imagine making love to her again and say, 'You are the only person I've been with apart from my wife.'

Pam reciprocates, saying, 'You're the first person I've been with in a long time and only the third person I've been with. I may be a little rusty.'

Knowing we feel the same way, she makes me feel at ease right away.

We both stare expressionlessly at each other while I'm kneeling between her legs. We both take a moment to appreciate each others naked body. I detect a fragrance that is a combination of sunblock, perfume, and her natural scent. I want to make sure she's pleasured before we make love.

I suggest something to Pam and she responds by gently nodding her head.

I allow her to bend her knees and spread her thighs while I lay on my stomach. I breathe in her lovely musk aroma before starting to stimulate her senses.

In order to observe Ethan's stimulation of her vulva, Pam lifts her shoulders from the floor. She feels tense as his tongue works on her sensitive area. Wetness and tickling sensations are felt as he uses his tongue and lips to stimulate her vulva and clitoris.

Her body begins to quiver as the sensation intensifies. She holds onto his head, indicating him to go deeper.

Her desire for him intensifies, and she can't spread her legs wide enough. She's never had a man do this before, so it's all new to her.. She quietly groans and squeaks as Pam feels vibration through her body. As she gets closer to orgasm, her body stiffens horizontally and her back arches.

I have to grasp her waist so she doesn't move as her body jerks away from my mouth. Her concentration is evident as she savors the moment with her lips slightly parted. Seeing her enjoy me and finding pleasure in it arouses me.

I miss the intimacy of being close to a woman and the way she tasted. I can keep doing this indefinitely, making her feel amazing about herself.

I perceive that Pam is about to climax, so I slip a finger inside her vulva to aid her. I softly caress along the warm, moist walls and observe her response.

Her natural aroma is beautiful and makes me desire her even more. The taste of her vulva is something I can't get enough of. I shift my focus to her spinster and swirl my tongue around it. My hope is that this will also arouse her and, based on her reaction, she seems to be enjoying it. Running my tongue across her hole makes her legs tremble. The flickering and poking inside was making her go wild.

While continuing, I slide my fingers inside her labia to push her over the edge again. I'm motivated to continue when I hear her squeal.

Pam's legs quiver with pleasure and she's not sure if she can keep going through multiple orgasms.

She's never had a sexual encounter like this before in her life. Ethan's ability to push her buttons effortlessly left her in disbelief. Pam presses her buttocks against his mouth, relishing the sensation of his warm mouth and gentle tongue on her anus. She has never had a man give it attention before until now.

Her body finally gives out and collapses.

Pam is no longer able to cope, and I can feel her body weighing on me. Using my hands, I support her thighs to keep her buttocks in position.

Despite her being satisfied, I continue to enjoy exploring between her vulva and anus with my mouth. From her deep breathing, I can tell she's exhausted.

Despite still finding it pleasurable, Pam pleads with me to stop. As I watch her struggle between wanting me to stop and not wanting the sensation to end, I can't help but laugh.

I pull away to admire her beautiful vulva and buttocks, taking in her lovely aroma without wanting to stop. If only I had entered her before, pushing her over the edge.

While We're Honest

♥

Pam needs the entire evening to recover from experiencing multiple orgasms in rapid succession.

She regretted not having a chance to explore Ethan's sexual prowess. Only for her to have him find out hers.

Despite being a widower with grown children, she was surprised at how adventurous he was. She underestimated him, expecting him to be average and conservative, but he proved her wrong.

I proposed we have ice cream and more wine to end the evening after spending a lovely time together.

I can't get over how good she tasted and how turned on I was watching her squirm and moan.

While we drink more wine and have fresh ice cream, there is no mention of earlier as if it is taboo, even though I wouldn't want to either. I had hoped she would say whether it was good or if there was anything else I could have done to make her feel even more great.

As thoughts swim inside my head, Pam goes to say something.

Pam tries to use innuendos to bring up the subject by saying, 'Wow, I needed this to cool off from earlier.'

I have no idea how to follow up on that and say, 'Well, I'm glad I was able to accommodate. I can understand how the ice cream can cool you down.'

Pam giggles at my comment as she takes another mouthful of dairy white ice cream and says, 'Are we friends or...'

I really want more than friendship and ask, 'What if I want to be more than friends? I think we are beyond friendship.'

Pam appears to be relieved and says, 'Phew. Thats what I want as well. Where do we go from here?'

I'm not sure what she means and ask, 'How do you mean?'

Pam seems to be all new to this and asks, 'Do we say we are boyfriend and girlfriend? Or dating?'

I smile and the idea of dating does not sit with me and say, 'I'm not up for seeing other people. And we both want the same thing. So, I would say boyfriend and girlfriend.'

We share a smile and a hug as I wrap my arms around Pam. We finish for the evening, go to bed and sleep right away without anything else happening.

The following morning, I wake up and am taken aback to find Pam awake, lying on her stomach with her elbows propping her up, gazing at me. Seeing her gorgeous smile, I can't help but smile back.

I wonder how long she has been up and ask, 'What did you wake up?'

Pam's eyes gaze at me as she says, 'Been awake about half an hour. Can't believe last night. Do you do that to all the girls?'

I try not to smile as I hear her laugh and say, 'Never did that with my wife. I can still taste you and smell you.'

Pam buries her head in the pillow as she goes embarrassed and muffles as she says, 'I can't believe you said that. Really?'

I keep a straight face and say, 'Yeah. You smell gorgeous and taste great.'

Pam pulls her head from under the pillow and blushes as she says, 'I feel bad for not returning the favor. I'm sure you taste great.'

I was not assuming anything and say, 'I was not expecting you to return the favor. I thought it was hot watching you getting turned on.'

Pam and I stare into each other's eyes without speaking. We examine each other's faces, appreciating our unique attributes and imperfections.

The idea of getting emotionally involved with another woman never crossed my mind. I didn't expect to be emotionally ready for a new relationship. There's an irresistible quality in Pam that makes me gravitate towards her without hesitation or fear of getting involved.

Pam sighs as she thinks about getting up and says, 'I should get out of bed and make us breakfast. You cooked dinner last night.'

I watch her climb out of bed with no clothes on and watch her cute bum wiggle as I say, 'I'll jump in the shower. We can stay in today.'

Pam turns her head and says, 'That would be nice. Maybe find something interesting to do.'

After smiling, she grabs her night top that she should have worn last night. It conceals her upper body and hangs just below her buttocks. She doesn't concern herself with underwear when leaving the room.

As she prepares a fruit salad for breakfast, Pam reflects on how sexy Ethan was last night. Imagining him setting her off again, she wished it was still last night. The thought of it makes her aroused.

Ethan was skilled at finding her pleasure zones, and she was surprised at how many times she orgasmed.

A huge smile appears on her face as she thinks back and almost laughs. Pam is experiencing sexual desires and is enthusiastic about having sex on the floor again.

Her mind pictures Ethan performing on her vulva while also making breakfast. Contemplating how much of a turn on it would be.

As I'm showering, thoughts of making love to Pam and the sensations of being inside her come to my mind. I think back to last night about how much I loved bringing her to ecstasy. Moreover, it was a surprise to hear her orgasm and to attempt to control her emotions.

The memory of her scent and flavor lingers, arousing me as I wash my phallus.

I am feeling an overwhelming desire to sleep with her due to the thoughts in my head. While she's preparing breakfast, I can see myself entering inside her from behind. Anticipating the sensation of her tightness and how quickly it will make me orgasm.

After showering, I put on a new set of casual shorts and a polo shirt. Take a look and see how Pam is getting along with breakfast.

Pam glances up when she hears me walking towards her and smiles as she goes over to the table with our morning meal.

As we sit together, she uses a ladle to serve fresh fruit into our bowls, as I watch her. Her top has me captivated, as I know she's not wearing anything beneath it.

Pam notices me staring and smiles some more as she says, 'I really had a nice time last night. I cannot stop thinking about it.'

I'm relieved she has reiterated her enjoyment of last night and says, 'Trust me. I would really love to do it again.'

Pam giggles and says, 'Yeah? Really? No regrets? After only grieving your loss.'

I smile behind my hands with my elbows on the table and say, 'I think I'm beyond grieving. I had no feel of guilt or sense of my wife around. Which I know sounds weird. But trust me when I say I stopped thinking my wife is here.'

Pam shakes her head and says, 'Thats not odd at all. It is quite sweet and endearing. Just glad you didn't feel guilty.'

I search my feelings and I have no loss in my soul anymore and say, 'I'm ready to move on. With you. I can see myself with you.'

Pam gushes and puts a strand of hair behind her ear and says, 'Good. I think the same. I can see us being together long term.'

We both stumble over our words and enjoy a tasty breakfast consisting of sliced orange, apple, and pear, along with pineapple fruit and juice.

The two of us are eager to continue where we left off once we're done. Following her towards the living room, I imagine what her bum looks like once more. In my mind, she lifts her top to show it.

While she walks, she pulls her top up slowly to uncover her peachy bottom and lifts it over her head. Then she discards it and turns to face me.

She stands there waiting for me to walk over to her. As we canoodle, I pull my top off and allow my shorts and underwear to fall to the floor.

Kissing passionately naked, we gradually kneel on the floor and she takes a seat on my lap. Her legs wrapped around my waist. We gently rock back and forth. She adeptly finds my phallus and gently manipulates it between her fingers and palm. My reaction is instant and I notice myself becoming more erect.

As she squeezes it, I feel my phallus throbbing in her hand and Pam gently squeezes harder to get me as stiff as possible. Next, she instructs me to open my legs and lean back with my arms behind me for support. I lay there while Pam positions herself between my legs and starts to move her tongue up and down my phallus, never breaking eye contact.

Watching her caress me makes me find her sexy, with my shaft coated in saliva. This feeling is wonderful and I've missed it for so long. Pam's tongue movements on the end of my length are causing an intense sensation that feels like it could burst out of my skin. Watching her delight in my response, I visualize myself reaching an orgasm on her nose and face.

I thought this would feel unnatural and struggle to enjoy her company. It feels like she has done this to me a million times, but in actuality, it's the first time. It feels completely natural and I love the sensation she is giving me. I'm not ready for this to be over yet.

Pam watches Ethan's body language to figure out what he enjoys during her first time giving oral. The way she approaches sex is heavily influenced by what she has seen and read in books and films. Eventually, she becomes immersed and quickly grasps what motivates him. Watching his face contort from pleasure arouses her.

She observes him go through the emotions and smiles occasionally, noting how happy he is.

My penis feels like it's going to explode due to the sensitivity after being circumcised. I spread my legs wider to give her more space to work on me. As Pam stimulates the nerve endings, my hips start to react with a knee jerk. My erection cannot grow any larger and is rock hard.

Pam seems to be relishing in the torment she's causing me as she maintains a tight grip on my shaft and works her tongue against the tip of my penis. As she continues to work me up, I can see her watery saliva cascading down my length.

Finally, I give in and cum surges out like a volcano, dribbling over her cute face and nose, but she remains unfazed. As she watches the thick flowing cream coat her hand, Pam almost laughs as she finds it fascinating. The amount that has flowed out has mesmerized her.

Pam approaches me and we lock lips once again. Passionately pecking each other's lips, we both share a smile and a laugh.

We find ourselves lying beside one another after the sensation fades, enjoying each other's company in silence. Holding her in my arms, we lay like broccoli savoring the moment.

Our bond feels even stronger the next day after last night. Pam proposes we walk around to find a cafe for coffee, breakfast and a chat.

We discover a restaurant about twenty minutes away from where we're staying and enjoy each other's company.

I want to discuss what we do from here since last night and say, 'Are you enjoying your smashed avocado and eggs?'

Pam finishes her mouthful and says, 'Yes. And your eggs and bacon?'

I smile as I respond by saying, 'It's nice.'

An awkward pause ensues as they both struggle for words.

I eventually want to broach the subject of us and say, 'Are we seeing each other now? Or was last night another one off?'

Pam smiles, not knowing the answer herself, but says, 'I'm not sure. It's up to you.'

I listen with my elbows resting on the table and my hands clasped against my chin.

I was staring down at my plate, worried by her answer and glance up from her response and say, 'Alright. I want to be a boyfriend and girlfriend. If that's what people still call it, these days. Or partner.'

Pam almost giggles as she smiles and says, 'Yes. That is what I want. I want to get to know more about you.'

I remember her mission and remind her to say, 'There is one problem, though. You're not going to be here much longer. You're going away.'

Pam knows, but she wants to pretend it is not happening and asks, 'What if I came back alive? Then, would that make a difference?'

I have an idea using my actuary skills and say, 'Based on historical data on war, there is a twenty-four percent chance of returning unharmed. A fifty-one percent chance of not make it back.'

Pam raises her hand to stop me rattling and says, 'I know. But having someone wait for me gives me hope I will make it back. Knowing I have you in my life will find me the way home.'

I touch her hand and our fingers intertwine as I say, 'I don't think I could lose another person again. But I can't see myself without you. So, it leaves me in a conundrum. I really like you.'

Pam makes it clear how much she wants us to be together by saying, 'I would be happy to go absent without leave. Get court marshall. If it meant having a chance of a real relationship.'

I can see in her eyes how much she means in her words and says, 'Well, I guess this means we're now boyfriend and girlfriend. Wow! How do I tell my daughters? Especially when she is a fight pilot. They will flip. In a good way.'

Pam smiles with delight and asks, 'Does that mean we can go back and be alone all day?'

I smile, saying, 'I guess it does. I'll get the bill. Let's go now.'

Being comfortable with each other, we are bare in front of each other. We stand inches apart in the living room, examining each other's bodies. The atmosphere is tranquil and motionless as we both enjoy this moment without wanting it to end.

As I run my forefinger along the side of Pam's body, she runs her fingertips across my chest. We can't believe we found each other.

I place my hand on her face and tenderly kiss her as she closes her eyes in anticipation. Now that we are together, it feels different not having to question if she has feelings beyond friendship.

Her hand wanders down my torso towards my length, arousing me instantly as she gently plays with it in her hand.

As she plays with it between her fingers, we continue to kiss fondly. My fully erect shaft is pressed against her torso.

While we were making out, she takes my hand and leads us to the kitchen counter. My eagerness to enter inside her is only surpassed by my observation of her curvy bum as I walk behind her.

Pam leans over the counter, signaling her desire for sexual intercourse. I kneel down and arouse her to ensure she's ready for me.

Ethan's soft tongue caresses Pam's vulva and strokes upwards towards her sphincter. Her bum hole being licked makes her unintentionally groan. She parts her thighs and lowers her hips to let him give her intense pleasure. Her sensitive nerve endings are easily accessible as he parts her pert bum cheeks.

She lifts her left leg and rests it horizontally on the kitchen counter as she feels the sensation intensifying. She intensifies the sensation by pushing herself against his face.

While stimulating her anus with his tongue, he pushes a finger inside her. Ethan's skilled work on her soaking wet vulva is arousing her more strongly than ever before, and she desires him to enter her immediately.

Wish We Could Disappear

♥

As I pleasure her vulva with my mouth, I softly stimulate my phallus to attain maximum hardness. The stunning fragrance of her aroma makes me very aroused. I'm ready to engage in sexual intercourse with her, as she's excited and prepared.

My rigid member slowly penetrates the damp and velvety inner walls. The moment I enter inside, I feel a warm and inviting atmosphere, and her scent fills my senses, making me even more excited. It fit like a glove, as if we were made for each other. We go together. Her tight vulva is causing me to feel aroused and want to climax soon. I initiate a rhythm to intensify the sensation.

The feeling of his shaft hitting the sweet spot inside her labia reminded Pam of how much she enjoyed it in Las Vegas. Every forceful movement fills her with immense pleasure. She removes her leg from the counter and clasps them together to enhance the sensation. She arches her back, allowing Ethan to penetrate deeper. The sensation of fullness overwhelms her after years without a man.

She gasps at the force of his length pushing into her. She feels sheer ecstasy flowing through her body, causing her legs to slightly wobble.

She eventually moves herself closer to him with her bum cheeks against his lower torso. Pam feels his strong hands on her shoulders as he thrusts against her bum cheeks. While arching her back and moaning, she motivates him to continue at the same pace.

I really want Pam to have a huge orgasm as I repletively thrust hard and fast inside her. I watch a film of sweat forming on her soft, smooth, tanned back.

Through the use of her vulva muscles, Pam tightens her lovely labia around me. The sensation is making me lose control, intensifying my circumcised phallus. I can imagine myself climaxing inside her any moment now.

I'm savoring her scent and the motion of moving in and out of her.

Pam wonders how Ethan maintains his stamina while she feels fatigue creeping up. She's reluctant to let go of the feeling as her emotions are on a rollercoaster ride. She could do this non-stop, experiencing his rock-solid length sliding in with intensity.

She thinks they are meant to be and complement each other perfectly. If only she had met this guy years ago.

Beads of sweat are dripping from my forehead as I watch my phallus slide into her hot body. My longing for her intensifies as I thrust harder.

Her groaning suggests that she's close to orgasm.

As her pert bum pushes against my torso, I move my hands around her soft and supple breasts to get better support.

Pam loves the way Ethan's big strong hands firmly grab her breasts and create a stronger impact entering inside her. As he thrusts into her, she rests the back of her head on his shoulder.

She's on the verge of climaxing on his breathtaking member.

It feels wonderful to smell the sweetness of her neck and hair. I wish this moment could last forever. The solid feel of her breasts and erect nipples between my fingers is an exhilarating sensation. The sweet aroma of her vulva is irresistible to me.

I feel my orgasm building up as Pam reaches hers. Our murmurs and groans are interchangeable.

Pam's orgasm surges through her body as she stiffens her back against his solid chest. She can sense his pulsating member ejaculating within her. He is breathing heavily after thrusting and gripping her supple breasts tightly.

He falls on top of her as her body collapses on the kitchen counter.

We came simultaneously, feeling a powerful sensation. I'm too fatigued to remove my phallus from inside her. We both breathe heavily after our intimate moment. We both laughed in surprise at how sexually charged we were.

Our hot, sweaty bodies required a cold shower after we had recovered. We don't shy away from discussing the excitement and thrill we experienced while making love. Pam reflects on how much she enjoyed the way I held her.

I express how much I enjoyed admiring her from behind and how lovely she smelled while we made love.

Joking about what we did felt natural and not strange. Our connection is so strong that it seems like we've known each other for years.

After showering, we put on fresh beach clothes and bask in the sun. We're unable to keep our hands off each other as we savor the remaining time here.

The guilt I once felt about being with another woman is now gone.

Pam now knows that my love for my wife is unwavering.

Pam wants to make arrangements after we get back, saying, 'I want to make plans when we get home. I have two more weeks and I want to have the relationship as if it is our last. I don't want to waste a moment.'

I'm glad we are on the same page and say, 'Thats exactly how I was thinking. I don't want to pretend we are just mates. I want people to know we are together.'

Pam plays with my hand while she smiles and says, 'Thats exactly what I want. I fancy going out on a good old date, like dinner at our local restaurant.'

I feel the same and say, 'Yes. But not your uncle's bar.'

Pam giggles as she finds my comment amusing and says, 'Sure. There is a great steakhouse.'

I think of last night's meal and say, 'Not another steak. I thought you would be steak'd out.'

Pam continues to intertwine her fingers in mine and says, 'Not totally steak'd out. I still want your meat.'

I try not to laugh but smile and say, 'Of course.'

The focus of the conversation turns to her demanding timetable. It seems Pam is lost in thought and distracted.

I show interest in what is on her mind and say, 'You seem sad. Having regrets?'

Pam quickly shakes her head and squeezes my hand as she says, 'No. The opposite. I will be leaving for my mission in two weeks. It is meant to be a one way trip. Only unmarried individuals without immediate family dependants were given assignments. It was fine four weeks ago. Before I met you. Now, I have a reason to make sure I make it back.'

I'm quiet and ponder as I listen to her before I say, 'Run away with me. We go somewhere where they cannot find us. We can live on several million dollars I have in one of my bank accounts. I'll take care of us.'

Pam smiles and then sighs as she exhales and says, 'That sounds wonderful. It is tempting.'

I hear a *but* coming and say, 'You don't want to disappear.'

Pam thinks about letting her pilots down and say, 'If it was one of them going absent without leave, I wouldn't blame them. But, I would feel guilty and not be able to relax. Trust me. I've found the man I want to be with for the rest of my life.'

I understand her reason and say, 'So, we head back to *Fallon*. Forget any more ideas about leaving. We get on the plane today and go back to our lives. We make the most of two weeks left of you being here. But I'm confident you will come back.'

Pam takes my hand and plays with it as she says, 'A part of me says yes and the other says no.'

I'm curious about the ratio and ask, 'Which side are you leaning towards?'

Pam is quiet at first and then asks, 'You want the truth?'

I obviously want an honest answer and say, 'Yes.'

Pam hesitates at first while she continues to entwine her fingers between mine and says, 'No. Which makes it hard to face reality that I will not have the opportunity to spend the rest of our lives together.'

I try not to be selfish thinking I will lose someone else again and say, 'Well, we better make the most of the last two weeks before I lose you. Live today like tomorrow will not come.'

I'm uncertain if she shares the same goal as me due to her disagreement. She made it clear that she wants to spend the rest of her life with me. I'm satisfied with that.

We finish by agreeing to forget about it for the rest of the afternoon and enjoy the remaining time in Cuba.

Pam and her colleagues are rehearsing another flight simulation scenario in the lecture theater on Monday before getting ready to fly.

Her thoughts drift to Ethan and their weekend together while listening to Buzz Saw. Their dinner together. Having passionate intimacy and spending time together. It brings a smile to her face.

The flight plan plays on the screen while Buzz Saw narrates and gazes at it. He checks if everyone is paying attention and realizes that Cougar is smiling and not paying attention.

Buzz Saw makes her jump as barks at her saying, 'Is something amusing Cougar? Something to share with the res of your team mates?'

Cougar snaps out of her daydreaming. as she is startled and says, 'No, sir. Nothing worth telling.'

Delta teases her, saying, 'Heard she went off base.'

Venom has one better and says, 'She got third base. By the way, she is smiling.'

Pam begins to feel embarrassed and wants to change the subject.

Buzz Saw quickly quiets them down saying, 'Thats enough. Cougar's personal life is not your concern. Maybe you should take a leaf out of her book. You have only got two weeks before you go on the unreturnable mission. Make the most of what time you have left. Do whatever you do to entertain yourself and what makes you happy.'

The lecture resumes by allocating specific roles to each team for the attack before they go up in the air and practice it for real.

The F18 jets have a virtual geographical layout of the land they'll fly over on their navigation system. Buzz Saw is having them rehearse the route so that their real flight feels like second nature. The last 14 days have been concentrated on achieving perfect timing for the contact drill. Eliminating the possibility of mistakes.

The toll of the G Force on their bodies and brains has left all eight of them exhausted. Hours are dedicated to repeating the exercise in the air until it's mastered.

Each time they repeat the exercise, the possibility of not making it back becomes more real.

Cougar's mind is consumed by thoughts of Ethan, and she yearns to see his face again. She has fallen hard for him and envisions a lifetime together. Their families blending and having fun with family engagements. As she flies back to base, she feels a multitude of emotions. Absent without leave is what she's contemplating to spend her life with him.

Expecting to be alone forever, she didn't mind being selected for the mission. Pam wishes she had met him months ago, now that she has a chance to find love and warmth in someone's arms. Meeting him earlier in *Fallon* would have made her ineligible for selection..

In less than two weeks, they will head to the *Philippine Sea*.

Pam calls Ethan on her cell phone after finishing her flight training and changing clothes. The urge to be with him is overwhelming for her.

She wants to plan a visit with her family and introduce Ethan to them. This will be the first time she brings a boyfriend home to meet the family. This is one of the items on her wish list that she wants to complete before her mission.

Holden and I are enjoying a beer on the garden porch while Amber prepares dinner on another hot, sunny day. Pam mentioning her conflict with Holden a few times has piqued my interest. My friend isn't the type to purposely upset others.

While we've been having a casual conversation about our day, I've been thinking about when to talk about him and Pam's situation. It's never a good time to bring up a sensitive matter.

I decide to just come out with it and ask, 'Why does Pam have animosity against you? She will never come over to meet me there. It is always meeting up at hers or a cafe.'

Holden does not appear surprised and says, 'I wondered when you were going to bring it up. You have spent so much time with her that I was expecting it to come up in conversation. There is more to it than a bitter hatred. She accuses me of causing her father's death.'

I'm blown away as she has never explained why and says, 'We didn't get that far. I didn't push the subject. I know her dad passed away when serving his country. How are you involved?'

Holden has no hesitation telling me and says, 'I flew with him. It was during the gulf war. We were on a reconnaissance mission. Filming certain parts of the region for threats and finding out their next strategy. Five recons in, end up getting hit by a stray missile. We never stood a chance. Teared clean off our tail wing. We naturally ejected and eventually touched down to earth. We were in the middle of nowhere. George, her father, did land so good. Damaged his ankle.'

As he tells me his story, I imagine it in my mind and ponder what he might have experienced. Losing his wingman has left him with a heartbroken expression. Seeing the pain on his face over what happened makes me feel sad. Pam would understand how difficult it was for him to lose her father if she could see him now. He has to pause to regain his composure before continuing.

I motion him to take his time and say, 'It's okay. I could imagine it was a like being in hell.'

Holden eventually continues and says, 'The middle of nowhere. Only a couple of hours before dark. The temperature goes below zero. With his foot, there was no way of walking outta there alive. He told me to leave him. But I went for help.'

By piecing together the information, I now know how Pam's father passed away.

Amber's call for dinner interrupts us, and we delay entering until my friend returns to back to his usual self.

Heading To The In-laws

♥

I have the complete story of Pam's father now. I'm considering whether to mention it during our conversations. I don't mean to be disrespectful, but I think she's being too hard on Holden. I would have done the same if I were in that situation.

If they had stayed there, both would have perished, so the only way to save them both was to seek assistance with a rescue. Move to higher ground in order to get a signal and radio in.

I feel like my girlfriend deserves to hear his side of the story. If she knew the entire story, she would understand and realize that nobody was to blame.

I asked Holden after dinner why he hadn't shared the full story with her. He informed me that it was confidential and he shouldn't have shared it with me. Since I had no connection with the Navy staff, I suppose he could tell me.

Pam and I have been going strong in a short amount of time. Since our trip to Cuba, we have been meeting up every night. Considering the time that may be left, this is particularly important.

With a week and a half until she leaves, I find myself counting the days. Every night, we've been intimate after dinner while discussing what we would do with more time.

Making every minute count when we're together.

Pam is taking a break from her training exercise today and she's invited me to meet her family. It will take approximately three hours by car to get to where they live, which is 150 miles away.

Pam is eager to introduce me to her family and has plans to bring us to her hometown. She has a better way of getting there, as it's too far for us to drive there and back in one day.

Upon my arrival at her place, Pam welcomes me with enthusiasm as if it's been weeks since she's seen me. After we hug, she checks to make sure she has her things.

While Pam is ensuring she has everything, I mention her animus towards Holden. In surprise, she stops what she is doing and slowly turns around.

I choose my words carefully before saying, 'I spoke to Holden a few days ago. Before you say anything, he told me without prying. I asked him if he found it awkward for us seeing each other, knowing you are avoiding him by not coming round to his house to see me. I know you don't want to talk about it and you find it hard to think about it. But all I'm saying is I know.'

Pam draws drops in disbelief and has an opposite effect when she says, 'You the whole story?'

I was surprised that she didn't get angry with me for thinking that I had meddled in her personal life.

I still act with precaution and gingerly say, 'Yeah. He told me in confidence and that it was classified. Again, I did not pry or make him tell me. More like he wanted to finally tell someone and let it off his chest. He was emotional as he told me.'

In a matter of seconds, her expression changes from surprise to anger and then curiosity.

Pam wants to know what was discussed and asks, 'What did he tell you?'

I'm not sure if I should betray my friends' trust in me and say, 'The total story of what happened to your father was told to me. But I owe it to Holden to respect his wishes. So, I'm at a conundrum.'

Pam's eyes dart around as she considers the importance and says, 'I don't want this to come between us. I like you. a lot. But knowing why he allowed my father to die alone to save his own skin is more important to me.'

It's the first time she informs me of her knowledge about her father's death. Besides, she has little knowledge of how he died and is strongly determined to uncover the full story. I experience some hurt when she easily dismisses our relationship and my feelings towards her. It rubs me the wrong way and makes me want to react.

I sort my words carefully before I say, 'I like you a lot. Even though this has only been a week. I have fallen for you hard. And, you want to trade this for my friend's side of the story? What do you know exactly?'

Pam is no longer threatening our relationship and says, 'Damn you. Using our relationship to protect a friend.'

I give a gentle smile and say, 'Touche. Only learning from you. What do you know and I will fill in the blanks? Without saying a word.'

Pam has a quizzical mind and says, 'All I know is his plane crashed. Holden knew where and didn't send for help. What were you told?'

I'm cryptic with my words and say, 'Part of what you said is true. But, the not sending for help is questionable. And you are missing something.'

Pam shows a gentle smile and goes on to enquire as she says, 'My dad flew with him. He took a missile for him.'

I find a way of correcting her and ask, 'Do you mean separate planes or a single plane?'

Pam quickly sees where I'm coming from and says, 'So, they flew together in the same jet. They both bought it. They were stranded together.'

The truth was finally known by her without uttering a word. I enable her to comprehend.

Pam's thoughts make realize she was wrong when she says, 'Holden did go for help. So, he didn't leave him to die.'

I gently shake my head and say, 'I didn't do anything. But, as a close friend, he would never leave a man behind.'

Pam smiles with relief and steps closer to me and says, 'Thank you. For finding out the truth of our my father died. Giving me closure.'

I wonder how she feels towards my friend now and ask, 'How will you be around, Holden?'

Pam appears guilty for the way she has behaved around him and says, 'Not sure how to face him at work now. It still hurts that nothing could be done.'

I have no advice to give her but say, 'Don't do anything. Pretend this conversation never happened. But look at him in a different light.'

She shakes her head in disbelief and smiles, struggling to believe that she knows how her father passed away in action. I stare at her buzzing inside for finding out the truth. Her happiness leads her to unexpectedly hug me tightly. Her voice reveals her gratitude, and this is her way of expressing appreciation.

Before leaving, Pam finishes collecting her stuff. I'm curious about Pam's reaction when she learns I'm taking Holden's car to drive us. Our plan was to drive to a farm at Pam's request and I was going to be the driver. There's something she wants to show me that's stored in a barn.

I strongly suspect that we will be flying since she's made it clear that she's not driving for hours to go to a family BBQ..

We had a brief conversation about her family and what to expect. I'm being honest, I have butterflies and it's been years since I had to meet my girlfriend's family.

Meeting potential in-laws again feels strange, especially when you thought it was only a once-in-a-lifetime event. I didn't imagine myself being with another woman, let alone meeting her family.

I'm curious to know what her relatives are like and ask, 'Are they expecting you with a new partner?'

Pam's mind is else whereas she stares out of the window and says, 'What? Oh. No. I don't want the day to be focused on us. They would have questions prepared and bombard me with them. This way, they will not have time to prepare.'

I have an idea she is nervous and doesn't know how her family will react, so I say, 'It is okay. If you don't want to say we are together, then just say we are friends. I gather you have never brought a boyfriend home before. Or they think you have never had a relationship.'

Pam grabs my hand resting on the gear stick and says, 'You seem to know exactly what I'm thinking. This is all new to me. I've never been in a situation like this before. I don't know how to introduce you.'

I find myself thinking the same with my family and say, 'I know exactly how you feel. I have never brought another woman back to my family. It will feel strange for me too. Not knowing if I introduce you as a good friend or my girlfriend.'

There's a shared understanding as we both smile, thinking the same thing.

Eventually, we drive off the main road onto a dusty dirt track bordered by fields and arrive at the farm. The barn is located a mile down the road, at the end of the track.

Pam tells me to park alongside the entrance.

We get out of the car and open the barn doors to go inside. I'm curious about what she has in store to take us to her family.

The barn in the unventilated causing a musky smell and dust particles are illuminated by the strobe lights shining through.

Pam heads straight to her plane, which is covered in a sheet of dust and has some strands of hay on it. Together, we removed the sheet to expose what was underneath.

There is a silver plane that has the ability to fly two people. If she had given me more notice, I'm wondering if getting on my plane would have been easier.

She needs my help to pull it out of the barn and face it towards the dirt track. There's no alternative space to use as a runway.

Pam has shifted back to being a pilot and is inspecting the wing and tail flaps, then the wheels.

Pam wants to ensure the safety of the plane before flying it, as it has been in storage for months. She ensures that the plane is not home to any small animals. Additionally, ensure the airflow is unobstructed by cobwebs or dust.

She views her boyfriend as valuable and wants to ensure his safety.

it is a restored World War 2 *P51B Mustang Fighter*.

As I watch her concentrate, I find her adorable and get the impression she's trying to impress me. There's something about Pam being in her element that I find sexy.

She completes her checks and tells me to get in.

She turns on the engine as soon as I take my seat in the back.

Smoke is coming out from the front nose of the plane. The propellor jumps into action, spinning at a high speed that makes it look like it's moving anticlockwise.

She secures the canopy over our heads while the engine idles with a chugging sound. I'm prompted to wear an aviation headset that's stored under the seat. She puts on a headset and I recognize it assists in communicating despite the engine's loudness.

Pam describes what she is doing by saying, 'I'm going to taxi along this dirt track. Hoping no one turns into this road. I need the whole road to take off.'

I have every faith in her and say, 'I trust your judgement. If you had told me you were taking me to see your family earlier, I would have sent for the company jet.'

Pam chuckles and says, 'My mum lives in the middle of no where. I don't think it would be appropriate to land a leer jet in the middle of the road. It would kind of give it away you have money. It is hard enough introducing you as my first ever boyfriend.'

I nod my head as I realize where she is coming from and say, 'I get it. Who is going to be there?'

Pam is backwards with coming forward and says, 'Maybe my three sisters. And their husbands and kids.'

I wonder what the ambient will be like and ask, 'Do they know you are going away?'

Pam does not answer straight away but then says, 'I thought it would be good to use this as an opportunity to see my family before I go away.'

As she thrusts the plane forward, our conversation halts and the acceleration forces us into our seats. The speed required for takeoff is achieved within seconds, just as a four-wheel-drive truck it turns onto the road.

Despite the sudden appearance of the oncoming vehicle, Pam remains unfazed and pulls back on the throttle, causing us to soar into the sky.

Glancing behind me, I notice the driver and witness the truck skidding to a halt.

Pam ignores the near miss as she concentrates on our flight plan.

Her mum's farm is situated along the southbound *Route 65 Veterans Memorial Highway*. The flight to the farm is one long, straight journey.

Once again, my girlfriend is flying me and the journey is giving me goosebumps.

I want to tell her how much I love being here by saying, 'This is great. This feels the closest thing to heaven.'

Pam giggles, agreeing and says, 'This is why I love flying. When I'm traveling at supersonic speed, I feel alive.'

While looking around, I notice the ground, small cars on Route 65, and the stunningly clear blue sky.

She directs my attention in the distance and identifies the named area of the landscape, as well as the popular cities of Los Angeles, Las Vegas and Reno that are located in certain directions.

I take in the tour and say, 'Wish we could do this every day. I can't wait to tell my friends I have a personal pilot who is a hot girlfriend.'

Pam laughs at my comment and says, 'You life is in my hand. I'll never let anything happen to you.'

I feel totally safe in her hands and say, 'There is nowhere else I would rather be. You complete me.'

It only takes an hour into the flight before we reach her mum's place and begin decent.

Approaching the farm on the private road, the landing is hard and a loud bang is heard, as if the wheels have busted.

Prior to landing, Pam warned me and assured the plane was in good condition.

Our arrival at the farm was after 11 in the morning.

Having landed safely and parked in front of the house, we disembarked from the *P51B Mustang Fighter*.

There's an abandoned feel to the house from the outside, with no sounds of animals or smells of BBQ.

The farm house is a well-maintained typical building.

Corn and wheat are being grown on acres of land. The house with faded white paint reminds me of growing up watching *Smallville*.

Pam can see how anxious I am to meet her family and rubs my back as she says, 'I got you. I'm not going to leave you alone for a second. I want to savor one more moment with them and have that moment of being with someone when I see them.'

I keep thinking there is time running out for us and say, 'We have to assume you will never come back. So, this couldn't be any more befitting. It is not worth assuming you have all the time in the world.'

Pam cuddles me and smiles to comfort and appreciate me. We finally walk in to meet her family.

Meet The Family

♥

Upon entering, nobody is visible inside, but we can hear noise from the back, indicating that everybody is outside. Before facing her sisters and mother, we squeeze each other's hands and push open the back door.

As soon as we walk out on to the back porch to the garden, her family fall silent and stares at us. I'm waiting for Pam to lead.

Pam hurries down the stairs to embrace her three sisters as her mother waits for them to finish bonding. I'm left at the top of the porch.

I wait for Pam to signal me to her family at the top of the steps.

The husbands of the sisters are conversing around a table in the garden while the children amuse themselves by running around.

The meat and vegetable skewers are almost ready and there are cooked burgers and sausages on the side. In addition to soft drinks, there's a selection of beers and wines available.

I pause, waiting for Pam's acknowledgement before introducing myself to her sisters.

Pam motions me over to show her sisters who she brought. With nerves and a smile, I accept her sister's warm hospitality. A barrage of questions come at me, making it hard to keep track and answer in sequence.

Pam is teased and they ask me what I see in their sister and how great she has been. I make it clear that my focus is on using her for air miles and free transportation. Her sisters find me amusing and laugh at what I say.

Pam's niece and nephew ambush her to play while her sisters take me to hang out with the guys. Watching her walk away with the kids, I envision her with children of her own. Children seem to come naturally to her.

Their husbands share a connection with me that makes me feel like family instantly. They inquire about my past and our first encounter. I'm open about my job, my late wife, and daughters with them.

Initially, they believe I am kidding about my riches, but when I show them my company website on my phone, they are stunned.

Show them pictures of my wife and kids and how they're taking care of the company while I'm gone.

It's a first for me to be able to describe who my late wife was and what happened to her without feeling pain or difficulty. They are compassionate and understanding, offering condolences. They then make a joke about pitying me for dating Pam.

To learn more about Pam, I ask about her from their perspective as a person. She has never dated anyone before, at work or outside, which is interesting to know. This confirms she was serious about never having a boyfriend. Her focus was entirely on her career, as she pursued becoming a fighter pilot to follow in her father's footsteps.

They question me as to why she chose me and I'm unsure. I can't explain it, but it feels like we were meant to gravitate towards each other. Initially, we were just friends but later realized our liking for each other.

Every now and then, Pam glances over at the table to see if Ethan is okay and wondering what they're joking and laughing about. Watching him get along with her brother-in-laws only increases her attraction towards him, and she wishes to overhear their conversation.

By the way, he handles the interrogation and keeps checking Pam, her sisters have given their approval.

Ethan has made a good impression on them.

It's late afternoon and lunch is ready on the table. We are currently preoccupied with savoring the mixture of meat and salad. We sit with our potential partners, gesturing and discussing embarrassing moments.

Pam's skeletons in the closet make the afternoon interesting, especially when she turns bright red. It increases my affection towards her and possibly my love for her. Out of all the people I've met in my life, her family is the easiest to get along with.

Shortly after the laughter subsides, I observe that one of Pam's nephews appears distant, gazing into the field a few feet away from us. I have a feeling that he's sad and I'm wondering why. As Pam and her family converse, I sneak off to investigate what was troubling him.

Quietly, I approach him and stand next to him, waiting to be noticed. He seems to have been crying and I stay with him, hoping he'll eventually open up. He eventually speaks out, questioning my reason for standing beside him.

I smile at him to make him at ease and say, 'I was minding my own business, admiring the landscape. Why are you standing next to me?'

John is his name, and he gazes up at me with a curious stare as he says, 'I was here first.'

I glance down back at him and say, 'Were you? I see you are not hanging out with the rest of us. Whats up kid?'

John shrugs his shoulder and says, 'Nothing much.'

I have an idea what it could be and pry by saying, 'Is it a woman?'

John appears surprised and gasps when he says, 'How did you know?'

I half laugh at him and pretend to make sure no one is listening and say, 'I guest. So, what's her name?'

John quietly opens up to me and says, 'Jennifer.'

I wonder what she is to him and ask, 'Who is she?'

John stares at the ground and kicks loose stones while he says, 'She is someone from my school. Not sure if she likes me.'

I think back to my childhood to relate and say, 'That happens a lot. Girls are a pain. They blow hot and cold. A bit like your aunt.'

John glances over at Pam and then turns to me with a puzzle expression and says, 'My aunt wouldn't mess anyone around.'

I try not to laugh at how small his problems are in comparison to life and say, 'I don't doubt you. But what about your girl? Do you think she blows hot and cold?'

John is in deep thought before he replies and says, 'I think she has gone off me. Not answering my texts.'

I offer and suggest saying, 'What if I contact her? See if she answers to me?'

John nervously comes to a decision and says, 'Here. Her number is there.'

After taking his cell phone from him, I type a message that says......

Another girl has shown an interest in me. Not sure how to react as I would rather be with you. If you are not interested, that is fine. I will get to know this other girlfriend, hoping something will come of it long term. If I don't get a reply, that's cool. Not expecting a reply as have not received response from other replies.

Once I finish writing the text, I show it to him before sending.

John's eyes open up, not expecting my idea, and says, 'I thought you were going to write how much I like her.'

I press the send button and say, 'You need to know if she likes you or not. Not asking her directly does not put her on the back foot or a knee jerk reaction. This way, if she really likes you, the girl will be a threat. If she doesn't like you in that way, it gives her a way out without feeling guilty for letting you down. Whatever her answer is, you will know she will be honest. The second girl gives her an exit without guilt.'

John sees me as some kind of goddess with women and says, 'You're alright. You know a lot about women.'

I almost laugh while staring at him in front of me and say, 'You'll get there. One day you will be giving your cousins advice as they learn about girls.'

Ethan and Pam's nephew are chatting, and Pam is staring at them, wondering what they're saying. She feels a warm sensation inside as she sees how well they are getting along. She observes his versatility in different situations. A man who can relate to her siblings and adapt to a nine-year-old boy.

She observes that their private conversation has ended and decides to join them.

In just a few minutes, John gets a message from Jennifer. His behavior is similar to someone getting news about their exam results. He wants me to see it and help him deal with the response, whether positive or negative.

While I'm about to read it, we hear his aunt coming over and I smile, happy for Pam's company.

I don't want John feeling embarrassed and say, 'This is a guy thing. Women aren't allowed.'

John backs me up and says, 'This is men only.'

Pam giggles, finding it amusing and says, 'You two boys are especially suspicious. I hope you are not leading my nephew astray.'

John stands up for me and says, 'Actually, he's been helping me out with a girl problem. You women are so complicated. Think he is a keeper.'

Pam appears appreciative how I'm blending into her world so easily. Also, seeing me giving her nephew advice on women.

I remind him of the text and say, 'See what it says.'

John anxiously goes the check in front of both Pam and I. We wait in anticipation and the smile on his face gives us the answer. To him, I am now a god and Pam is proud of how I've made her nephew happy.

It's getting late and we should head back now.

Among everyone here, Pam and I have the farthest to travel home. We have to return to base before the gate closes for the night.

We're both mindful of the time and hastily express our need to depart.

Standing up too quickly, I feel a little light-headed and slightly wobble. I sneakily move away from the picnic table, thinking nobody noticed. I was mistaken, and her family was quietly laughing at me.

Pam finds me amusing, but rolls her eyes when she sees how much alcohol I've had.

Her mother promptly asks if we need to use the bathroom before departing. We think it's best to check if we need to go, just to be safe.

While ascending the stairs inside the house, I express to Pam how much I enjoyed myself and how fond I am of her family. I can tell she likes what I'm saying from the way she's gushing.

Pam grabs me and kisses me against the wall as we reach the top of the stairs, something I had been thinking about all day.

I can't fully enjoy the moment when I'm feeling lightheaded and wishing to be sober while making out with her. Despite not being myself, she still enjoyed our brief smooch.

We finally make it to the bathroom and check if we need to go.

Pam went first as I waited against the wall opposite the bathroom door. Every time I shut my eyes, I feel myself drifting off to sleep.

After a few minutes, Pam comes out of the bathroom and leaves the door open for me to see if I need to go.

As I try to decide if I need to go, I find myself gently swaying and falling asleep. Pam inquires about my well-being, as it's been a while.

Hearing her tap on the door wakes me up and I come back out.

We kiss intimately again, even though she knows how drunk I am. It does not make her like me any less. It does not worry her that I may make a fool of myself.

It amuses her seeing me drunk and is more concerned I will be okay flying back to Fallon. Pam thinks I'm adorable when I have had a few drinks.

Eventually, we walk back down stairs to see ourselves off with her family.

When we get back to the party, everyone has wondered why we were so long. We are both embarrassed, not wanting to explain what we were doing.

We spend twenty minutes saying goodbye to her family and heading back to the plane.

One of Pam's siblings shows their approval of her choice in man. Speaking for the rest of the family, they see him as a great catch. They wonder how she managed to meet someone with her closed off life.

Her sibling was not sure if Ethan was joking about his financial background. But Pam sets the record straight by saying he owns an insurance company and has his own leer jet.

She sees in his eyes how much the realization sinks in.

A smile comes over his face as it sinks in more, knowing her boyfriend is a multi millionaire.

I'm still surprised how welcoming they were and how much they made me feel like one of them. If Pam was not going on her assignment, I would have liked to see them again. I really like her family and felt like I had known them for years.

Being grilled by her sisters was interesting when we were just friends.

While I thank them for the food and drink, Pam nags at me to get going, as it is late. Her family gang up on her, telling her to leave me alone. We are encouraged to stay over, but we have other plans tomorrow and I know Pam wants me to herself.

As we walk to the plane, they decide to come with us, so they can see us fly off.

It is still daylight at nine o'clock in the evening and feels like six o'clock. The day was great and simple, spending it with her side of the family.

Now the alcohol has had time to take its effect and the fresh air, I feel really drowsy and drunk. I almost stumble, getting on the wing to climb inside the back of the cockpit. Her family giggle seeing me in the state I'm in.

I have to concentrate on getting back into the cockpit. Laughing to myself does not help, as I feel embarrassed.

Pam rolls her eyes as she helps me in, but she is smitten with me and finds it funny seeing me drunk.

Her bum is so sexy as I watch her crouching inside.

The engine comes and on and her family and friends cheer after the propellor begins to spin on full power. Pam and I wave them goodbye as we head for the end of the road to allow for plenty of distance to take off safely.

Before we take off, the engine roars loudly while we speed along the ground, anticipating the moment we reach 15 miles per hour.

While speeding by her family, we saw them wave at us as we suddenly became airborne..

The L Word

♥

Pam thanked me for coming along and said that they enjoyed my presence, assuming that we were a long-term couple. With a drunken, happy feeling, I laugh it off.

As we fly high in the air, heading back to *Fallon*, I can't help but admire the view of the sky around us. The color of the sky is so captivating, I can't get accustomed to the scenery. The sky displays a mixture of yellow and orange, along with a dark brown cloud line. Without a reference point, it's difficult to determine how fast we're moving.

Being up here feels peaceful, away from the busy crowd below. It feels like we're the only ones on earth. The sun has disappeared behind the sky, indicating that dusk has arrived. The plane's wing shines as we soar pass the golden orange sun.

As we move towards the north, the sun sets in the west, to our left, and it creates a serene atmosphere. I feel like I'm near heaven up here and I think of my wife for a moment.

I sit in the back of the P51B Mustang Fighter with my thoughts, enjoying the peaceful silence. When I reflect on my wife, my attention is drawn to Pam and the depth of my feelings for her. The idea of losing someone I cherish is a painful thought.

I wonder if meeting people who won't be in my life for long is a jinx. I wonder if I'll outlive those around me.

I had such a good time today; I don't want to lose her. I envision a future with her, possibly even marriage.

Watching her fly us to see her family is so sexy. I feel secure in her company and believe she can do no wrong.

Pam calls out to me through the headset above the engine's noise while I'm lost in thought. Hearing her through the headset is something I can't get used to. Her voice sounds hoarse and is loud, which the communications system causes.

Pam wonders what I thought of her family and asks, 'Did my family scare you off?'

I half chuckle and smile as I say, 'They were interesting.'

Pam wants to know what I was talking about with her nephew and asks, 'What were you and John talking about?'

I smile as I think back to the conversation and say, 'There is a girl he likes. Was never answering his calls. He was paranoid she was not interested.'

Pam laughs and smiles at the thought and asks, 'So, how did you reassure him?'

I tell her what we discussed and say, 'A text gave the answer. Simply told her he had another offer.'

Pam smiles while she rocks her head and says, 'I was worried you would be overwhelmed and freak out with the interrogation.'

I always knew they would be keen to want to know about her love life and say, 'I would have found it weird if they hadn't. I'm the first guy you took home. And not the usual boyfriend. They know I was married and widowed? With three kids?'

The conversation turns to the formation of a beautiful dusk.

Pam's voice almost quivers as she has thought and says, 'This always feels like heaven. I sometimes think my dad is looking down on me from up here. Making sure I'm okay.'

I make light of the situation and say, 'Yeah. Is your dad giving you approval of your choice in man?'

Pam does not respond to my comment and asks, 'What about you? Does this make you feel closer to your wife?'

I'm surprised she thought of her and say, 'I was thinking about her earlier. I do feel she is here. But for her to see, I've moved on and no longer wallowing inside. Also, to let her see I met you.'

Pam appears smitten by my words and says, 'I will never replace her. And I will never stop you from thinking of her. I think I can see us being together forever.'

I have the same thought and say, 'I cannot imagine being with anyone else.'

While making small talk, we come across a murmuration of birds that cross our flight path. We didn't have time to avoid it, so we plowed right through the middle of the pack.

Pam shouts out, saying, 'Bird strike! Hold on. We are going down!'

The wings of the plane are covered in feathers and the canopy glass cracks within seconds. The engine emits a loud whirring noise and then smoke appears. A faint smell of cooked bird is detectable.

The propeller battles to maintain its spin, obstructed by feathers.

The engine sounds like it's about to stall and Pam is struggling to maintain control of the plane.

Although we could be in danger, I feel at ease with Pam at the controls.

Pam manages to stay composed as she considers the different probabilities of outcomes. She fears her one and only relationship might be brief.

The engine starts to splutter and fail, forcing them to glide through the air. They can only hear the wind and feel the nose of the plane dipping down.

Pam is determined to keep their romance from being short-lived in a plane crash.

Despite the need to panic, I remain calm and accept whatever fate has in store for us. I'm content with where I am and have no other accomplishments to strive for.

Pam grits her teeth while grappling with the plane and says, 'We are going down. Fast.'

I believe in her and say, 'I have faith in you. Whatever happens, there is no other person I would rather be with.'

We are descending rapidly at great speed and the ground seems to be getting closer to us. My ears feel pressure and intense pain. I observe Pam's frantic behavior as she fearlessly attempts to restart the engine during our descent towards the ground.

The engine stutters a few times before coming back to life. Pam operates the controls to pull us out of a spiral dive.

Pam fights for control of the plane while her thoughts keep going back to how much Ethan means to her.

Her actions cause her heart to race as she feels the plane responding.

As the plane approaches five thousand feet, the nose begins to level off. Gradually, her relief shows as she maneuvers the plane to a horizontal position and diverts danger.

The incident left us both shocked and reminded us of life's brevity. In order to be safe, a touchdown away from residential areas takes ten minutes.

Pam made certain she landed in a farm field, to avoid any fatality.

The wheels hit the ground with a bang and I wait for them to explode. It'll take a few minutes to reach a stationary position due to the bumps along the dry, dusty field.

We both feel relieved to step out of the cockpit and touch the ground. As we laugh in shock, my thoughts turn to kissing her.

Pam swiftly checks the condition of her P51B Mustang Fighter for airworthiness while I ponder our return to base. I examine my cell phone and contemplate a masked signal, wondering who to reach out to.

She seems unsure if we can fly and appears deflated based on her expression. I find myself more attracted to her after surviving an air crash together.

Pam sighs as she stands in front of the plane and says, 'We should be able to take off at first light. After clearing the feathers from the propellor and wings.'

I notice there is a barn in the distance and say, 'We can use that place to get a night's sleep. Then come back for the plane in the morning.'

Pam glances over and considers it a good idea as she says, 'Yeah. Let me sure her and then we can go over.'

We need to use our weight to open the large doors of the barn, which takes a couple of minutes. The farm equipment inside includes a tractor, plow, and hanging tools.

Stacked bails of hay are surrounded by strays of straw covering the ground.

I think out loud, saying, 'It's doable.'

Pam seems to be fine with it and says, 'We can jump on top of the of those piles of hay.'

Seeing Pam in her element as a pilot makes her even more sexually attractive to me. The only thing I can think of is making love to her after a near-death experience.

As we approach the hay stack, I keep my eyes on Pam's back. I suddenly feel the urge to grab her from behind by her waist. Turn her around with force and press my lips against hers. She pulls us apart briefly and examines my face, concentrating on my eyes, skin, and mouth before throwing herself at me and wrestling with each other.

It feels like we've been kept apart for so long and now we're finally together. Pam and I both lack patience in ripping each other's tops off while breathing heavily.

Our hands were all over each other and we stumbled into the hay with her back against it. I lift her up and throw her on top, and then climb up after her.

As I climb on top, she greets me with a smile and looks into my eyes. As I remove my pants, she's encouraged to take off her bra. Then I remove her jeans and underwear.

Pam can't take her eyes off of Ethan's manly chest with some tight curls. She observes him as he slowly inserts his phallus inside her and feels every centimeter of it. Memories of their earlier encounters flood back as she gasps.

Her near-death experience made her more aware of how fortunate she was to have him in her life. She wouldn't have died alone. Holding onto him as if tomorrow may never arrive.

She dug her fingers into his back as her vulva muscles tightened around his length.

Encouraging him to push harder by squeezing his bum cheeks.

With her hands on my bum, pulling me closer, I push harder with each thrust. During lovemaking, I gently suck on Pam's earlobes, which she enjoys. When I listen to her, I find her soft and quiet groans cute.

The sweet scent of her hair and great perfume on her neck is noticeable.

As Pam nuzzles into his neck, she can't help but notice the pleasant and luxurious scent of his aftershave, which she adores. As he caresses her earlobe with his tongue and lips, she reaches a climax.

The cool air inside the barn causes her body to stiffen as she shivers through multiple orgasms.

Ethan desires to continue without having reached climax yet. She proposes trying rear entry to increase his sexual stimulation.

Lying on her stomach, she waits in anticipation for him to slide back inside her. As he enters her, she pushes up and arches her back. She crosses her legs and tightens her vulva muscles, hoping it will help Ethan reach climax.

Another wave of electricity shoots through her body as she keeps stimulating him, resulting in a second orgasm. She moans out loud and clutches at the straw involuntarily.

As she experiences another orgasm, I feel her tight vulva grip my hard length. With two more hard thrusts, I finally release myself and cum heavily inside her, spurring me on. Then crumple onto her. Sweat beads on my forehead while her back glistens with perspiration.

I withdraw slowly since it's highly sensitive, shuddering as I completely exit and lie down beside her. As I hold my arms around her, Pam shakes a little after I pull out and we spoon together.

We peacefully drift off to sleep.

When I woke up the next morning, I realized that Pam wasn't there and I was lying naked in the dark with light streaming through the cracks in the wooden barn's walls.

I hurriedly search for my clothes and get dressed. Head towards the barn door and walk outside to see if she's close to her plane.

It appears that her plane is almost clear of feathers when I look at it from a distance.

Pam senses me and turns around with a smile when I'm a couple of feet behind her. I'm wondering how long she has been up and spent time removing the feathers.

Pam checks the propeller and the engine to see if there is any obstruction still and says, 'You finally woke up. Good timing. We are almost to ready to test this baby and go home.'

I browse the size of the field, seeing if there is any other life, and say, 'Has the farmer come out?'

Pam continues to show concentration while checking the plane out and says, 'Farmers round here are used to seeing strangers land in their field. We will be ready to leave in another five minutes.'

Once again, the sky is bright blue, and the visibility is fantastic. I sit on the back of the wing. I'm thinking about how hungry I am and I wish we were nearby a café or tea shop.

Pam sees me staring into space with my mind occupied and says, 'I had a really nice time last night. It's weird what your life flashing before your eyes can do. It has made me like you even more.'

I motion with her and continue to see beyond the field and say, 'I love you.'

Pam was not sure what she heard and ask me to repeat when she says, 'Say that again.'

I close my eyes and breathe in the fresh air through my nose and say, 'I love you.'

Pam stops tinkering with her plane and says, 'You love me.'

I stay in the same position with my back to her still and say, 'Yeah. I'm thinking we should go for dinner to celebrate not dying.'

Pam does know how to react and says, 'You surprise me every day. I wish I knew what love was. I have never come across it before. But, I really like you. I don't want to be with anyone else. And I would have rather died with you than anyone else.'

I smile after hearing her answer and I'm happy. At some point, she'll realize what love is and make up her mind.

With her finished, we can finally leave.

Invited To Dinner

♥

Pam flies us close to the ground during takeoff in case there are any more bird flocks in our way. The sight of the plane's shadow beneath us brings back a sense of peace.

We're both lost in thought, content to let the silence linger.

Ethan is all Pam can think about, and she doubts she deserves his love. She thinks it takes six months to fall in love, and they have known each other for only three weeks.

She longs to know the feeling of love as she searches her feelings for him. For her, love means growing old together and desiring to be married. She desires to spend every moment of the day with him and wishes to spend the rest of her life with him. Her mind is consumed by Ethan every day and cannot focus on anything else. The thought of having children with him crosses her mind, and she envisions him as a father to her kids.

She feels privileged that Ethan chose her to fall in love with. Pam does not perceive herself as special and values his love for her.

I feel like I've lived a complete life twice, and it's proof that love can be found again. Your love does not have to resemble your first, second, or third love. Mimicking the notion of having the same affection for Pam as I had for my wife would be weird.

I have come to understand that it's acceptable to move forward and seek new love. I'll only upset my wife if I ever try to compare her to Pam or see if my love for her is better than the love I still have for my soulmate.

I'll be okay if things don't work out with Pam, since I've already had the privilege of experiencing it. I love Pam and I believe in living each day to the fullest because life is too short to suppress your emotions.

I'm going to adopt this new perspective on life and share it with my daughters, assuring them that no one can ever take their mother's place. I'll keep the photos out for display and only add new ones to the shelf.

We reached *Fallon*, which should have taken twenty minutes, but it felt like only ten minutes of traveling. Once the *P51B Mustang Fighter* is inside the barn, we cover it with a dust sheet. As I approach the car and open the driver's side door, Pam surprises me by grabbing me for a passionate kiss. It seems like we both had an emotional weekend and share the same feelings.

Pam eventually pulls away and says, 'I really had a great time. The best bit was spending the night in the barn. You do know there is no one else I want to be with. And it is not your money.'

I already know and joke with her when I say, 'It is the way I kiss you.'

Pam smiles while she shakes her head and says, 'No. You are an awful kisser.'

I rack my brain to what it could be and say, 'It is the aftershave I wear.'

Pam continues laughing and pecking me on the lips as she says, 'Nope. You aftershave is mediocre.'

I think of something which makes me smile and say, 'It's the size of my... jet.'

Pam tries not to laugh while are lips and locked together and eventually says, 'Yeah. That is it. If you didn't own the jet, we wouldn't be together. Seriously, it is the way you make me laugh, the way you kiss me and maybe the jet. That is fun to fly.'

Eventually, we get into the car and I drive us back to her place.

We go inside her place and she makes us coffee. As I waited for Pam, I texted Holden that I was okay and informed him that we had to stay overnight. I didn't elaborate on last night's events, but I ensured him it was a spontaneous decision.

He replied that he didn't think much of it and assumed we would sleep over at her family's place.

Pam wonders who I have been texting as she passes over my cup of coffee and asks, 'Is that Buzz Saw?'

I have to think at first and then realize, as I say, 'Yes. Holden. You'll be seeing tomorrow.'

Pam reminiscence our conversation yesterday and says, 'Yes. It will seem strange seeing him in a different light. Thank you Ethan.'

I shrug it off and say, 'I wanted you to know the truth. If it was me, I would want to know if I was going to face my death. One thing cannot do is choose who you want to love. I meant it. Running away. I can take us anywhere in the world.'

Pam thinks I'm sweet and gives me a peck on the lips and says, 'I know. It is another reason why I really like you. I will come back. Because I have you waiting for me.'

As we sip our coffees and look at each other, I realize that I will have to return to Los Angeles soon. Staying here would be great, but my priority is taking back control of my company.

We had dinner in the evening and talked all night about the barbeque and recovering from the bird strike after losing control of the plane.

After a couple of days, I noticed my daughters were texting me more frequently and urging me to return to work. I won't return to work until Pam departs for her mission. Their exchange of messages resulted in them securing a private jet to fly to *Fallon*.

It is another weekend with two more weeks left with Pam before she goes away.

Today, in the afternoon, they will arrive and rent a car to reach Holden's house. They want to see why their father is not coming back to Los Angeles yet.

Already told Pam they are coming and want them to meet her. She will be joining us for dinner tonight, along with my daughters and the Holden family. I'll be cooking dinner and bringing drinks for us.

There's a large pot of chili that I'm cooking, which contains fresh tomato, garlic, sugar, and canned ingredients. At the moment, it's simmering and waiting for the rice to finish boiling. The chilli beef contains red peppers, so I'm having fresh cream to reduce the spiciness.

Holden and his family will be home soon, and so will my daughters. Pam is expected to arrive at six, which is when we're planning to have dinner.

The reality of the situation is causing my nerves to kick in. Pam is going to meet the most significant people in my life. I'm anxious they could think she's not the type of person I should be with or that I should be with a woman who has a more conventional career.

When I hear the door open, I can tell which of the kids it is by the sound of their footsteps and vocalization. Luke walks into the kitchen to find the source of the delicious smell of food. When he tries to taste my cooking, I softly hit his hand with a spatula.

Luke quickly moves his hand after getting it smacked and says, 'Ow. I just wanted to see how it taste. What is the special occasion now?'

I tell him about leaving soon and say, 'My daughters are coming over to find out when I'm going back.'

Luke's interest is peaked and says, 'It's going to feel weird you not being around. You made these last six months interesting.'

I will miss being here too and say, 'This was my second home. It will feel weird waking up my own bed.'

Luke kind of gets slightly emotional and says, 'You'll come back right. We've gotten used to your expensive wines and beers.'

The door sounds once more, and the assumption is that Emma has returned from University. Rushing in with enthusiasm, the person wonders what dinner will be. She becomes suspicious and wonders what the special occasion is.

Emma wonders why she gets to enjoy my cooking again and questions about the origin of my culinary skills.

I strain the rice once I check one of the grains is soft, as I say, 'My daughters are coming over and so you will be able to meet them.'

The doorbell rang, and it has to be either my girlfriend or daughters. As it becomes real that my daughters will meet Pam, whom I'm in love with, I ask Emma to open the door, feeling more anxious.

I can hear faint voices from the kitchen, but besides Emma, it's hard to tell if it's Pam or one of her daughters speaking. Since they're taking a while, I head to the front door to check who it is.

As I approach the front door, I notice my three daughters having a casual conversation in the living room. As I walk in, my three daughters stop what they're doing and stare at me.

It looks as though Shona and her sisters Naomi and Jordan just came from work, given their attire of suits. The paperwork they brought requires my signatures.

Shona is slim, with light skin and straight hair that fall to her jawline. She is in her early forties. She stands at five feet and seven inches tall with a slender, curvy physique.

Her wardrobe consists of dark colored two piece slim knee length suits paired with expensive high heel shoes.

Her life revolves around work and enjoying spare money, without any serious relationships.

Naomi, with thick palm tree-like curls, filled out cheekbones, and fair dark skin, is in her thirties. She is five foot six inches tall and has a slender physique.

Her outfit consists of a knee-length skirt, blouse, and flat shoes in light colors.

She is married with two children and maintains a work-life balance in her personal life.

She isn't driven by work and doesn't hold a senior position in the company. Despite owning a stake in the company, her work does not have an impact on its performance.

Jordan, with relaxed hair that falls down to her shoulders, has high cheekbones and slightly darker skin, and is almost thirty. She has an hour-glass figure and stands at five feet six inches tall..

Her suit and shoes are similar to Naomi's.

Currently, her attention is on work until the time is right to seek love and start a family.

Shona has been casually questioning about Emma about my well-being to gauge if I'm prepared to return to work. It appears from her body language that she's eager for me to come back to work and take charge of the company.

I call out the elephant in the room saying, 'I will be heading back in a couple of weeks. As you can see, I'm back to myself. I needed this time away.'

Jordan wonders who I'm seeing and says, 'Emma tells me you've met someone and been on several dates.'

I feel awkward about being happy with someone else and say, 'It nothing serious yet. She is going off to do a tour and I'm heading back to LA. So, it will fizzle out before I get a chance to really know her.'

Naomi wonders about if things were different and asks, 'If she was not going away and you were to stay here, what would happen between you?'

I shrug my shoulders, but deep down I know the answer and say, 'Maybe settle down with her.'

Holden and Amber's arrival causes a distraction, taking the attention off of me. The only person who hasn't arrived yet is Pam.

While waiting for her arrival, I introduce my daughters to them and they quickly become acquainted. Making them aware the three of them are involved in managing the company where they work.

I watch them ask about my work behavior and whether I've been a nuisance or overstayed my welcome. Making light of the situation and laughing conservatively.

The doorbell sounds, and everyone eagerly anticipates Pam's arrival.

Around the table, ten of us are feasting on my chilly beans and rice with salad. The family welcomes my daughters and shows interest in knowing my real self.

Pam's smile and the laughter around the table are the only things I focus on, enjoying the evening. With a glass of wine in hand, I observe Pam's interactions with the Holden family and my daughters from my seated position. I can't decide if Pam would be a good match for my family when she comes back from her trip.

Pam's behavior was unusual as she laughed more than ever and found her quite cute. She even had her hand on my lap and periodically glanced in my direction to check on me. While laughing loudly, she squeezes my thigh and falls into my chest.

I come back to reality and attempt to participate in the conversation. The conversation is too crowded to join in. The Holden children are participating in the discussion as well.

I assist Amber with clearing the table after dinner while they remain in conversation. I assist with loading the dishwasher.

Amber sees how withdrawn I am and says, 'I guess it is too much. Having your family here and hoping Pam is accepted.'

I give a surprised expression and say, 'I pictured it one way and it's going a different way. I thought it would be me having to get the conversation going. But, I wasn't needed.'

My eyes are fixed on the counter as I concentrate on listening to her.

Amber smiles and says, 'It not for you to make your daughters like her. And it is up to you to decide if you want her as a part of your family.

I can see they really like your girlfriend. They approve. And I can see how Pam feels comfortable around the table and she adores you. I can see in her eyes how much she loves you and vice versa.'

My ear perks up when I hear her say, Pam loving me.

I wonder how she can tell and say, 'She has never been in love. She said she doesn't know if she will know what love is.'

Amber continues to smile and says, 'It's not what you say. Anyone can say they love you. But your actions are what tell a person they love you. Her love language was checking on you to see you are okay. And the way she dotes on you.'

I never noticed being focused on everyone getting along and say, 'She flies out in a week. And she could be gone forever. It is unlikely she will return.'

Amber encourages me to have hope and says, 'Make this week as if it is your last.'

Our conversation is halted as one of her kids enters the room.

Last Supper

♥

We are done for the night as it's already eleven and it's too late for my children to return to LA. They are provided with sleeping bags and the living room to sleep in. Pam decides to sleep over and shares the room with my daughters.

The rest of us go to our own beds.

The following morning, everyone had showers before a late breakfast. We're having another lighthearted chat.

By mid day, Pam, my children and I are left to our own activities. The moment has arrived to go over some documents that need to be signed.

Pam observes Ethan and his children heading out to the backyard to show him some documents. Seeing him in his element uncovers another aspect of his personality to her.

His posture and mannerism shift as he peruses the papers, ultimately drawing big wavy lines at the bottom of the pages. His emotions are concealed while he flips through stapled paperwork and signs at the back.

As Ethan signed his name with theoretical swirls of the pen, she couldn't believe how cold he seemed. While his daughters discuss business issues, he shakes his head in a calm manner.

Pam is intrigued by how he can easily switch from being playful to serious.

Ethan catches her observing them and briefly smiles before reverting to his serious demeanor.

After finishing the pile of documents, the subject changes to discuss office politics within the company. There's whispering going on among the staff regarding my return.

We finally go to sit down and there are enough chairs on the decking for all of us to choose a seat.

I wonder how things are and say, 'Tell me how things are going.'

Shona takes the lead and says, 'Everything is fine. Certain senior manager is feeling comfortable taking orders from a woman.'

I ponder in silence and say, 'I'll be back in a week. I can make it official that you sisters are collectively CEOs. I will see to the general day-to-day stuff. But you three run the company.'

They seem unsure if I still have my faculties, with their mouths open.

Naomi, not being career driven, is not sure if she wants the responsibility and says, 'I'm happy with what I'm doing now. I like having time with my family.'

I see her worry and say, 'Hence why the three of you will be running it. So, neither of you will be giving up your life.'

The three daughters are content with their new role and responsibility. My aim is to reduce work and focus on having a companion. Begin relishing life.

Jordan is hesitant, but speaks on behalf of her sisters and says, 'I assume Pam is the reason behind this. We are happy you have found someone to keep you company. She seems nice. Is it serious?'

I notice all three pairs of eyes are poised for an answer and say, 'It's only been four weeks. And she flies out next week. There is a small chance she will not make it back. So, it is not related to her. But your mother and Pam have made me realize how short life is. It is time to sit back, but I won't be resting my feet up. I'll still be coming into the office to do menial work to keep the mind ticking.'

Naomi appears to be sad to hear my decision and says, 'You're not going to be one of those dads who finds a girl half his age and squander half your fortune.'

I feel insulted and say, 'She is a similar age to me. Pam doesn't care about how much money I have. I have no interest in meeting anyone. Pam happened to come into my life.'

Shona wonders how we met and asks, 'Where did you meet?'

I almost laugh and say, 'We did not meet. I walked into a bar and she was working behind it. I still had my hair style and beard. She thought I was some kind of surfer or bum. I wasn't exactly wearing my two thousand dollar suit.'

They soon come to understand how rational I am and how well-planned this is. They realize that I've given my life a great deal of consideration.

Pam keeps observing, questioning if they're discussing her. Her hope is that they are not discrediting her.

Holden creeps up behind her and says, 'Worried they will not like you. Keep him apart from you.'

Pam tries to hide to her worry and says, 'We only have a week left before I no longer see him.'

Holden forgets about how their relationship is strained due to him be responsible for her father's death and says, 'Surprised you came since you hate me. Does he know you are going on a no return mission?'

Pam feels her eyes becoming watery and rubs them as she says, 'No. He thinks I have a chance of making it back. But he has already given me a probability. He's an actuary. Spends life calculating the odds.'

Holden faintly chuckles and says, 'He knows. But he is being hopeful.'

Pam thinks about the truth of how her father died and says, 'Don't have a go at him when I tell you he told me what you told him.'

Holden slightly smiles and says, 'That was to supposed to be between him and me. I never assumed he would tell you.'

Pam smiles to herself and says, 'I assumed that. Why couldn't you tell me the truth?'

Holden takes his orders seriously and says, 'It was classified. Who do you think helped with your career? Out of guilt not saving your father. You think you're that good?'

Pam smirks to herself and says, 'I know I'm good. Why do you think you asked me to go on the mission?'

Holden has worry on his face and says, 'It was not my idea to send you. I tried to get them not to include you. But, you are best who will be leading the team.'

Pam continues to keep her eye on him while conversing and says, 'If I'm going to lead us, I want to give them a chance to say their goodbyes to love ones. The day before we fly out.'

Holden wonders who they will give their goodbyes to and says, 'The whole point of recruiting them is they don't have family.'

Pam senses they do and says, 'Everyone has someone to say goodbye. Make it happen.'

Holden doesn't agree, but he will do as she asks and says, 'I'll see what I can do. So, are we good?'

Pam remains silent and shakes her head slightly.

I've answered all my daughters' questions about my future plans and sanity. The knowledge of their future has brought them relief. Now that they're satisfied, I can go search for Pam.

As I approach, I observe Holden and her ending their conversation and becoming aware of my presence. As I approach them, Holden moves away.

Pam smiles when I approach her and says, 'Hope it was all good.'

I give her a short version and say, 'They were worried I was losing my marbles. Giving them the reign of the company.'

Pam wonders what I will do and says, 'I assume you are still going back to Los Angeles.'

I find it more real thinking out loud and say, 'Yes. When you leave, I'll be going. Thought we could go out for a nice meal before you leave.'

Pam likes the idea and says, 'I would love that. I would like to see you every day until it is my time to leave.'

I was thinking the same and say, 'I was thinking the same.'

Our conversation is interrupted by my daughters letting us know they're ready to head back on their flight. I offer to give them a ride to the private jet. Pam went home and organized to meet at her place after my daughters fly away.

Upon arrival at Pam's place from the private airfield, we couldn't help but feel the urge to make love. We keep going until almost midnight.

We spend every possible minute together for the rest of the week, making the most of the time we have left. In the days leading up to her departure for the *Philippine Sea*, we made love almost every night.

We had a positive discussion about what to do when she returns from her mission. I vow to take her to the best places in Los Angeles and spend more quality time with my daughters. Pam assured me she would teach me how to fly and get my pilot's licence.

By making plans, we hold on to the hope of seeing each other again. Pam often reminds me how much she values our time together and wishes we had met in a different era. She ensures that I hear everything she wants to tell me.

We've been really honest about everything so that we don't regret anything if we don't see each other again.

As requested, Pam and her team are given a day off before flying out, but she can't wait five minutes before calling Ethan.

Pam feels giddy, like a teenager on their first date. She's feeling butter-flies in her stomach, just like when she first dated Ethan. She's filled with ideas about what they could do tonight. They can relax, as they don't have to wake up early tomorrow. Spend the day and evening free of work-related thoughts.

Spending one more day with Pam for the last time makes me fill with dread. Simultaneously, feeling thankful for spending a complete day with her for the last time.

Pam gave me a spare key so I could make dinner for us before she comes home. I prepared a meal from my family's traditional recipe called Pepperpot. It's a black sauce that marinates beef or pork, and I chose beef. *Cassareep*, a thick sweet sauce made from *Casava Root*, is delicious. Additionally, I've cooked rice to accompany it and the bread roll is perfect for soaking up the sauce.

I haven't eaten this dish since my wife passed away, but I think Pam will like it. This will be her last meal before risking her life behind enemy lines.

Prior to my visit, I packed my things at Holden's and planned to leave at the same time as Pam. Packing my clothes away in my suitcase felt strange. I observed the clothes Pam selected for me during our time in Las Vegas.

Plates and cutlery are set on the table, with a pepper pot in a china bowl and a separate bowl of rice. While pouring myself wine and waiting, the door goes, and it's perfectly timed. Pam's face lights up at the sight of me cooking for us.

I pour her a glass of wine and get myself another one. Watching Pam taste the wine, she's pleasantly surprised and assumes it's an expensive bottle based on her expression.

My ancestral meal was so enjoyable that we both had seconds, leaving hardly any meat and rice left. The fresh bread rolls are perfect for soaking up the sauce. Pam shows she is full by sighing and slouching in the chair. Reading her appreciation for the meal and company brings a smile to my face.

With the TV on, we snuggle on the couch and finish the wine. I have a feeling that Pam is reflecting on our relationship and worrying about our separation after tomorrow. Her somber expression indicates that she's fully present, living in the moment. We have a mutual under-standing without verbal communication.

While she faces the TV, I stroke her hair and relish the scent of her skin and hair. I am present in the moment, cherishing every minute with her.

Pam's voice quivers as she turns to face me and says, 'I don't want to go. I want to stay here with you.'

I watch a single tear cascade down her cheek and say, 'I'm not going anywhere. I will light a candle to show your way home. If you want to run away, I can have twenty million wired in a few minutes and find a private jet somewhere. Choose a country where twenty million can go far. We never work ever again. Pay cash for everything.'

Pam touches my face and gives a partial smile as she says, 'I would really go with you, but my team needs me. I don't think they stand a chance of making it home without me. I'm the best pilot going.'

I wish she was not good at her job and say, 'I wish you weren't a pilot, even though it is sexy and has its perks.'

Pam tries not to laugh and says, 'Make love to me. Right now.'

We rush into her bedroom and hastily undress. We cannot keep our hands off each other and our lips are unable to unlock. It is like the first time we are making love.

Pam lies on the bed, anticipating my arrival to make love to her. I intend to make Pam's night unforgettable by kissing her affectionately and taking my time to fully satisfy her.

As we kiss passionately, I gently caress her breast while gazing into her eyes. I stimulate her by placing her nipple between my fingers and gently twist. I can tell she's getting sexually aroused by the hardness of her nipple..

A few minutes of nipple stimulation and sucking makes it rock solid. As I tease her with my tongue and gentle bites, I hear her murmuring in response. Her groans signal her readiness for me as I keep stimulating her.

Placing her arm across my back, she motions me to keep going and I follow her cues.

Pam is aware that she will miss how Ethan adeptly listens to her subtle sounds. She finds it arousing when he gently tugs at her nipple with his teeth. Ethan pushing his finger inside her vulva, causes her to flinch and pant softly. Gasping, she feels it roughly sliding in and brushing against her clitoris.

She widens her legs to help Ethan delve deeper inside her and expertly guides him to her sensitive area.

Goodbye My Lover

♥

Ethan was able to generate enough friction to bring Pam to orgasm once more, sending her over the edge. As her back arches, Ethan doesn't stop and continues to stimulate her sensitive area, leading to waves of pleasure.

As tidal waves of pulsating spasm take over her, Pam digs her fingernails into Ethan's back.

He observes her response, listening to her heavy breathing and watching her mouth unable to speak. His face lights up as he observes his girlfriend experiencing pleasure and enjoying the moment.

Ethan is amazed at how much he has pleased Pam, and he notices that the bedsheet is now damp. After some time, he withdraws from her soft and lubricated vulva, taking a brief moment to appreciate the sweet musk scent.

As Pam laughs at how fantastic the experience was, she thinks Ethan has really surpassed himself this time.

As she reaches for his rigid phallus, she aims to satisfy him. Her arousal seems to have had an effect on him as well.

The sensitivity of Ethan's circumcised length almost makes him jump when she strokes his phallus. Pam observes it while she plays with his throbbing girth. She notices a vein running along it, which she hadn't before.

She motions for him to lie down as she slides down the bed and delicately wraps her lips around his firm erection.

As I lay there, I close my eyes and sense the texture of her tongue. I find it arousing and stimulating when her mouth creates suction. Cupping the base, Pam uses her tongue to slide along the length of my shaft. Every now and then, I feel her soft lips on my testicles as her hand moves along my phallus and gently squeezes the end.

After a few more minutes of stimulating me, she began to properly masturbate me. While working on my orgasm, she lies next to me and turns me on with her kisses.

Due to my circumcision, I'm very sensitive down there, causing me to wriggle my body. As I react to the touch of her hand, Pam finds me amusing and smiles. Despite that, I still enjoy having her lips on my mouth.

I love the feeling of her soft warm palm jerking me while her breasts press against my chest. It's fate that we should be together. We fit together perfectly and it feels so natural to be with her.

While nearing orgasm, I squirm as the sensitivity increases and Pam realizes my phallus pulsating. She smiles, almost laughing, and speeds up her rhythm, knowing I'm close to orgasm.

Unable to contain myself any longer, I suddenly released a rush of liquid that cascaded over Pam's fingers, prompting her to laugh at how relieved I must have felt. She was surprised by how much I spilled and I apologize for the mess on her hands. She was amazed by how much came out, but assured me it was okay and enjoyed making me reach climax through foreplay for the first time.

After she finishes, I watch her rub my mess onto her bedsheet.

After we've both recovered from our separate orgasms, we can finally make love, and I'm interested in trying a different position. When I suggest something, Pam giggles and says she's up for new things.

Pam positions herself on her belly and arches her backside upward. As we awkwardly move into position, I try not to laugh. While standing over her, I slide my shaft vertically into her vulva with care. I bent my knees to lower myself against her beautiful bum.

We both find a comfortable rhythm and enjoy the new position, while Pam feels me going in deeper.

Pam gasps as she feels every inch of his phallus slide deep inside her and finds the sensation overpowering. Wishing she had thought of it herself, it feels great. She signals Ethan to quicken his pace as his shaft stimulates her clitoris more intensely.

Ethan doesn't need any more encouragement as he presses himself as hard as he can against her bum while he builds up momentum. Pam feels his hands moving towards her breasts and finds comfort in him using them as support.

He tightly grasps her memory glands as he thrusts himself fast and hard into her. In order to intensify the sensation, she tightens the muscles in her vulva to grip his shaft firmly.

This is a wonderful feeling and we should have started doing this weeks ago. The sight of sweat forming on her back is a huge turn-on for me. While holding her supple breasts firmly, I enjoy the sensation of her smooth, flawless skin rubbing against my cheek. As I maintain a fast pace, I feel another orgasm coming on.

Both of us vocalize how close we are to reaching orgasm. I ejaculated first, and she followed shortly after.

She feels his thick sperm flowing inside her as his throbbing phallus brings her to another climax. While riding the waves of her orgasm, her legs shake and convulse uncontrollably.

Unexpectedly, he slides out, and suddenly she feels his mouth on her vulva and his tongue sliding along her sensitive skin up to in-between her bum cheeks. The sensation of his hot breath on her skin and his tongue exploring her crevices brings her pleasure. He is so spontaneous that she can't believe it.

Ethan swirls the circumference of her spinster. He finds it strange yet thrilling sensation.

I don't know why, but I felt like giving her oral and savoring her scent after sex, and appreciating her attractive physique. Making the most out of the time remaining. I am cherishing every moment with her today, knowing it may be the last time we are together.

I want her to always remember me and what we did together, so this is my way of ensuring an everlasting memory.

We stayed up until three in the morning, carrying on well into the early hours of the next day. They engaged in sexual activity three times, with foreplay and oral in-between each session.

When I woke up around eleven o'clock, Pam had already been up for quite some time. As I wake up, she greets me with a smile.

She made breakfast for us both and carried it into the bedroom with a smile. I shift in bed to receive a tray holding scrambled eggs and toast.

The memory of last night keeps replaying in our minds. We were trying hard not to laugh at how much we enjoyed each other's company.

I feel like going away for the day and ask, 'Why don't we spend the day somewhere else? Maybe go to Las Vegas again. If we had more time, go back to Cuba.'

Pam goes into deep thought and says, 'I don't want to have thoughts of wishing I was not going on my trip tomorrow. I would definitely feel like running away.'

I know where she is coming from and say, 'You're right. I would think the same. So, what do you want to do?'

Pam touches my hand and stares me in eyes and says, 'Just want to stay here. Savor this moment. Spend time together with no distractions. This is what I want to remember, if I don't see you again.'

I respect her choice and say, 'Okay. We can sit here. Savor the moment and create a memory of enjoying time together without the distraction of traveling, strangers in the crowd, and occupying our minds with making plans. We can sit on the sofa or stay in bed in others arms. And make the most of now.'

For the first time since we've been together, it feels strange not to do anything. We're not doing anything, just sitting here in silence. Pam finds comfort resting her head in my lap while lying here. It seems to me that she's having difficulty accepting that we may not see each other again.

Until she leaves, nothing feels real to me. Only then will I experience what she is currently going through. It feels like I will see again tomorrow or next week.

At nine o'clock the next day, Pam has to leave for deployment. She will be flown by helicopter to her aircraft carrier. Her task is scheduled for Saturday at ten in the morning.

The weather is hot and clear blue skies once again. Pam takes us to the location where she and her colleagues have been waiting to be collected. We stand at a distance of a few feet from the runway tarmac's edge.

The sound of fighter jets taking off and landing fills the air as they commence and conclude their training exercise. The sound of planes flying overhead is constant, like we're at a commercial airport.

Each one of them has a packed naval bag for the trip. They've placed them on the grass next to themselves.

The navy light brown uniform trousers and shirts are being worn by them with a white T-shirt underneath. They appear relaxed as if it's an everyday routine. As if they are not going on a dangerous trek.

While waiting, Pam and I embrace each other. Holden has arrived in his uniform to go with them. He will be observing them from the communication room in the aircraft.

Where we stand there is no protection from the sun or anywhere to rest.

The helicopter arrives a few minutes later and lands gently, taking its time.

Pam waits for everyone else to board before getting on herself, even though she has her bags with her. Pam turns towards me and I notice tears in her eyes, causing me to feel emotional and uncertain about how to say goodbye.

I wrap my arms around her without any prompting and give her the strongest hug, not wanting to leave. Pam's grip is just as strong as mine, and neither of us wants to let go. My eyes water uncontrollably and I can't seem to stop myself from being emotional. I didn't anticipate feeling this way.

In an effort to avoid being spotted by her team and Holden, Pam tries to control herself and act brave while we share a quick kiss.

I urged her to go and watch as she climbed inside the helicopter. Watch the *MH-60S Sea Hawk* slowly ascend into the air. The pilot makes a slow exit with a half-circle turn. I stay until I can no longer see the helicopter in the distance. When it's no longer in my line of vision, I prepare myself mentally to return to Los Angeles.

I won't have the freedom to see her whenever I please anymore. The pain in my heart is dull, as if someone I love has died. It's hard for me to believe she feels the same since her mind is consumed by the mission she must undertake. She had to concentrate on safely bringing her people back after a perilous journey.

I booked a cab after she left, and now I'm in the back seat, reflecting on what we had. The driver attempts to engage in small talk to break the silence, but I only partly pay attention and respond minimally.

I'm not feeling very sociable right now. I just want to be alone with my thoughts of us and remember our time together. I smiled as I remembered the laughs we shared and how amazing our lovemaking was.

I met her quirky family and they welcomed me with open arms, treating me as if we had known each other for years.

The time she attempted to impress me with her culinary skills, only to burn the entire meal. I chose to treat us to dinner instead. It's those moments that put a smile on my face.

During the flight back, I keep replaying the same memories in my mind. I put my forefinger under my lower lip and stared into space. On our way to Las Vegas and Cuba, I couldn't help but stare at the chair she had sat in. If she were here right now, I wonder what conversation we'd be having.

As I leave the private airport in the next taxi, I start to feel anxious about returning to an empty house without my wife and now Pam. I'm imagining the front door being blocked by a plethora of mail. I wonder if my wife's presence still lingers in the house through her scent, or if time has allowed it to fade away.

I feel like something is blocking my way as I enter the house and make my way through piles of junk mail like magazines, newspapers, and envelopes. It's been seven months since I last came here, hard to believe.

I close the door behind me and close my eyes as the reality of losing Pam overcomes me. I'm alone again.

Cougar, Razor, Storm, Delta, Trojan, Venom, Enigma, Pulsa, Lobster, Fox, and Buzz Saw, who now go by, are heading towards the aircraft carrier.

Throughout the journey, Ethan was all that Cougar could think about, longing for his company. It has assisted her in avoiding thoughts of her task and her responsibility to ensure her team returns home safely.

She spent the journey trying not to cry as she looked out the window to avoid being seen.

Upon boarding the ship, they receive a final briefing below deck.

Condors Away

♥

The debriefing room resembles a lecture theater, with a walkway running through the center and five rows of seats on either side, similar to a cinema. A whiteboard at the front has a projector fixed to the ceiling, displaying a flight simulation terrain of the area they will be flying through.

Moving forward, the pilots will be referred to by their call signs.

Buzz Saw reiterates what they have been training for over the past six weeks and says, 'This is it. You will fly below radar past *South Korea,* which will be your three o'clock flying over *East China Sea* into *Jiansu* and from their continuing West.'

After observing the map, Cougar notices that there is mostly farmland further inland. Her assumption is that they will mainly fly over rice paddy fields. The target can be reached by taking a route with a deep valley that can provide cover.

Buzz Saw stands next to the whiteboard using a pointer to assist his speech and says, 'You will use the hills on either side of the valley to go in undetected. The rough terrain will prevent any ground threat. It will take an hour, cruising at two hundred miles an hour.'

From memory, cougar recounts her training and visualizes what will appear next on the projector.

Buzz Saw goes to bring up the diagram of the plant and says, 'The last few miles of reaching the target, you will fly over flat land providing no cover. You will fly out of the valley, leaving you open to any threats. Here, the fun will be begin.'

On the whiteboard, Cougar sees the plant that she recalls from when she was first recruited for this kamikaze mission. The plant is half the size of a football pitch and has a square form. There is a surface-to-air missile on the roof of the plant.

Sandstone is the primary material used to construct the building, which also has dark brown metal girdle doors.

There are a couple of armed soldiers and some engineers inside. The plant has a fuel tank and computers that analyze and read the plane's computer.

The jet is fully operational, but it has undergone testing by two pilots.

Buzz Saw gives an update of what intelligence knows and says, 'Once you are out in the open, you will be seven miles from the target and surface-to-air missiles can pick up threat six miles away. They are Russian *S-75 Dvinawill* which can reach you before you get anywhere near the plant.'

Razor speaks up to affirm the situation when he says, 'It is a dog fight with missiles. We get past them, we destroy the plant. With what left we have after using our weapons on them.'

Buzz Saw waits for him to finish talking before he says, 'This is what you have been trained for. By the time you face the first four missiles that pick you up, another twelve will follow. What you will have are five lots of twenty counter measure flares, missiles and bullets. There will be thirty flares, twenty-four missiles, and six hundred bullets between you. You are the best. You will make it home.'

Cougar pictures what might take place when those missiles are triggered. The challenge is to eliminate them and then get to the building to take it out.

Buzz Saw continues and says, 'When up in the air, Cougar and Storm will be condor 1, Venom and Enigma Condor 2, Trojan and Fox Condor 3, Razor and Delta Condor 4, and Pulsa and Lobster Conder 5. Condor 3, 4 and 5 will provide cover triggering the *SAM* and leading the missiles away from the factory. Condor 1 and 2 will hold back staying more than four miles away from the *S-75 Dvinawill's*. When you see the *SAMs* are clear, you fly in and take out the target. As your wingmen head out and back home, Condor 1 blow the doors open and Condor 2 takes out the asset. Then all five of you head back home.'

The room is silent as the pilots take time to process the task.

Trojan wonders if there will be sea support and asks, 'Will you be providing cover as we near our missile range?'

Buzz Saw does not show encouragement when he says, 'Our tomahawks have only a range of one thousand miles. You will be traveling eight hundred miles over sea and then three hundred miles across land. That is over one thousand miles. You will be alone.'

Cougar thinks that will not be all and says, 'The explosions will echo for miles. We will attract attention.'

Buzz Saw already assumes this and says, 'It is likely you will come across *Chengdu J-20* jet fighters. They are faster than our *F/A-18F Super Hornets*. Which means you bolt out of there at supersonic speed. Don't even stop for the bathroom.'

The room falls silent again at the thought of having to face the *Chengdu J-20's* and *S-75 Dvinawills*.

The thought of being with Ethan is more appealing to Cougar than facing her daunting mission.

Razor affirms again saying, 'So, when we survive the surface-to-air missiles, blow up the building with the aircraft in, it is a dog fight with *Chengdue J-20's* all the way home. With no support. Okay, got it.'

Buzz Saw shows no expression as he observes his elite team and then says, 'You have trained for this. You are the best. Now, get suited up and ready to deploy in thirty minutes.'

Buzz Saw watches them leave the debriefing room as indistinct chatter about the mission fills the air.

He quickly takes hold of Cougar to keep her while the rest depart.

Buzz Saw wants to talk to her to make sure she's at peace with the truth about her father's death. Cougar was surprised when she was pulled aside unexpectedly..

Cougar has a confused expression and asks, 'Is there something you want?'

Buzz Saw is not subtle when he says, 'I was wondering if everything was fine between us and about how your father died.'

Cougar wonders why he would be interested and says, 'We are good now. Why are you concerned?'

Buzz Saw wants to make sure she has no stone unturned and says, 'In case you don't make it back, I want you to have closure and be at peace.'

Cougar contemplates the success of the mission while changing into her flight suit. Portraying the result while pondering if she'll reach home.

As she changes, she ponders whether her destiny will mirror her father's. She has Ethan to ensure she arrives home safely.

She zips up her jumpsuit while absentmindedly gazing into the void.

The tannoy comes to life, asking her and the other pilots to board their jets.

All pilots are ready to launch from the aircraft carrier and go into dangerous territory. They are naturally anxious and waiting for the green light to go. They depart in two minutes, counting down. There is silence as they wait.

Cougar casts a glance at her colleagues, hoping for their safe return. Then, she fixes her gaze on a picture she had with her. There's a photo of Ethan taken during their Las Vegas trip.

She has a photo of Ethan that he's unaware of, and it's caught on the edge of a groove on the control panel in front of her. She delicately runs her fingers over the picture.

Buzz Saw is currently in the Combat Information Center, waiting for his team to deploy and put their intense training into action for the real attack mission..

A navigator is in charge of giving commentary on their location and warning them of any dangers.

Cougar observes the crew on the flight deck in their distinct colored jersey tops while waiting for take off. Their movements resemble those of farm ants, who appear to have no apparent coordination. Every crew member has a duty that is connected to the person next to them. The flight deck crew wears different colors to distinguish their positions and duties.

Cougar and her seven other naval aviators must observe six colors while inside the jets. The jersey tops come in white, brown, blue, red, green and yellow.

The white jersey officers have inspected the four jets for the mission. To ensure they are safe for flight.

Cougar and her team will be directed to the short taxi run by officers in brown jerseys for takeoff. The condors will be directed in numerical order, and Cougar will be the first to deploy from the aircraft.

The blue jersey officers work under the supervision of the yellow jersey officers as trainees.

The task of purple jersey officers is to make sure that the five jets are fully fuelled, which can allow them to travel up two thousand miles.

Red jersey officers are available if there's a fire or an exploding jet during landing. Cougar and her team don't plan on using them.

The green jersey officers will activate the catapult, enabling the five jets to deploy from the aircraft carrier by achieving the required speed.

Officers wearing yellow jerseys will indicate to the five pilots when the launch of the catapult will occur.

The pilots must now position their aircraft, guided by the yellow jersey officers. The five fighter jets are arranged in a sequence, with Conder 1 taking off first.

The officer in the yellow jersey is waiting for the officer in the green jersey to signal that they are ready to press the catapult button.

With poise, cougar waits for the yellow jersey officer to signal with an arrow-like hand gesture.

She remains observant of the yellow jersey officer, waiting for their signal to depart. Blue flames are bursting out from behind with the after burners on full power.

Once she spots the arm extending, she salutes, and the catapult launches her forward. In mere seconds, she jerks forward with force, exits the aircraft carrier, and ascends into the distance.

The navigator watches the radar and gives Buzz Saw an update accordingly.

The navigator begins commentary and says, 'They are now being deployed. Condor one, away. Condor two away. Condor three away. Condor four away. Condor five away.'

Buzz Saw intently gazes at the radar screen, spotting five jets as dots with a line displaying their code names en route to their destination.

Leading her team across the *Philippine Sea*, Cougar is comfortable heading towards *Xishui County, Hubei*. They will arrive in four hours, traveling at a speed of three hundred miles per hour.

The journey from the carrier to the coastal line of China takes three hours, followed by an hour through a valley flanked by high mountains and forested terrain below.

The fighter jets fly in a diamond pattern over the ocean, undetected by radar, but visible on satellite images from their aircraft carrier.

Upon reaching land, Cougar commands her team to adopt a single file attack formation. All respond in numerical order.

Condor 2 Venom acknowledges and says, 'Copy.'

Condor 3 Trojan says, 'Copy.'

Condor 4 Razor says, 'Copy.'

Condor 5 Pulsa says, 'Copy.'

She can hear her breaths through the mask, using this to distract herself from the mission. She occasionally looks at the picture of Ethan that's stuck next to the altitude indicator.

The jets in the distance can be heard by the natives in the region. As they work in the rice paddies, they immediately look up and watch foreign planes fly overhead.

After a brief moment, the fighter jets were gone, and the farmers returned to their rice cultivation.

On the other side of the valley, there are clusters of civilization that react like Mexican waves to the loud noise of low-flying fighter jets. The jet engines' roar startles the birds in trees, causing them to disperse from the branches.

Condor 1 Cougar and Storm, Condor 2 Venom and Enigma, Condor 3 Trojan and Fox, Condor 4 Razor and Delta, and Condor 5 Pulsa and Lobster are on the verge of reaching the other side of the valley.

Before flying over the flat plains, there is a steep climb to make that is almost vertical.

Cougar takes the lead and says, 'We approaching the last leg of our journey. Once we fly out of the valley, we won't have anymore cover. The surface-to-air missiles have an engagement range of four miles. We have another three hundred miles once we go over the ridge of the mountains.'

Each one pulls their joystick and flies over the mountain, just a few feet above the surface. In succession, each pilot flips their fighter jet onto its back, pointing the cockpit towards the Rocky Mountains.

Upon scaling down one side of the mountain, they turn the jets upwards and maintain an altitude of under three hundred feet. As they approach their target, they maintain their single file formation in flight.

Below them, there are additional rice fields where farmers are hunched over and wading in water up to their shins. They hear a loud noise and instinctively stop what they're doing to investigate. The sound of five fighter jets fills the air as they pass overhead, followed by a gust of wind that makes the long, thin grass sway.

Farmers find noisy gas guzzling planes to be a nuisance that interrupts them. They shake their heads in disapproval of the unnecessary noise.

They are almost at their destination, and less than one hundred miles away. There's a sense of quietness and emptiness in their location. They seem prepared for trouble even though everything is going smoothly. The calm prior to the storm.

Cougar makes sure her team does not get complaisant and says, 'Keep your eyes peeled. Don't get relaxed. We are almost within range of the surface-to-air missiles. Remember your roles. We will be moving into attack formation soon.'

Razor, Pulsa, Venom and Trojan copied, then went silent again.

Buzz Saw has been monitoring the radar screen closely. The temperature of the room seems to have increased due to the intensity of the mission's anticipation.

Comms officer has been keeping regular vocals of their position and says, 'They are now fifty miles from target. Still doing three hundred miles an hour. Not long now.'

Buzz Saw remains silent and doesn't engage the officer in conversation.

Inside the plant, there are three engineers who are testing the final particulars of the aircraft, which is a clone of the American prototype.

They're making sure the instruments accurately measure the jet's speed. Today, there's a planned test run.

Three soldiers were deployed to protect the engineers and secure the jet's safety.

The plane, which can only travel for fifteen hundred miles without refueling, has not been refueled yet.

Two pilots are given the task of testing the plane to see if the problem has been solved by the engineers.

You need to travel for thirty minutes to get to the main road from the plant.

In case of an attack, the surface-to-air missile detection system is connected to the building alarm and will activate the yellow sirens. Afterward, there's a lockdown.

The soldiers need to manually activate the communications radio to call for outside assistance. The location requires a half-hour drive for a small army to get there.

Two fighter jets will be dispatched to the site within 5 minutes of the plant alarm being triggered.

Condor Down

♥

The *S-75 Dvinawill* range can detect them at a distance of just under six miles, so it's time to prepare for the attack.

Cougar begins to get nervous and says, 'You know what each of your tasks are. Get in attack formation, with Venom behind me. We are about to face a storm.'

Fox examines the radar for any bandits and says, 'It is clear. Prepare for the *S-75 Dvinawill*.'

Pulsa feels something is not right and says, 'Lobster, keep heads up. Those missiles will jet off with four miles of activation range.'

Cougar now knows she must keep her distance away and says, 'Venom. It's time to pull back and allow Trojan, Razor and Pulsa to take out the *S-75's*. Good luck.'

Again, the other fighter jets respond in numerical order.

Condor 2 Venom acknowledges and says, 'Copy.'

Condor 3 Razor says, 'Copy.'

Condor 4 Pulsa says, 'Copy.'

Condor 5 Trojan says, 'Copy.'

The remaining trio of jets stay on track and brace for the approaching *SAMs*. They are nervous and eager to finish this.

The *S-75 Dvina sprang to life upon detecting the three F/A-18F Super Hornets within its six-mile radius*. The base made a loud whirring sound as it slowly turned to face the three fighter jets in the east. As the four missiles take aim, the platform tilts and prepares to launch when the fighter jets are within four miles.

Once the yellow sirens start flashing and a deafening ringing noise echoes through the plant, the alarm is triggered. A soldier from the trio uses the radio to call for help and air support.

Amidst the chaos of the alarm and frantic engineers, the missiles launched with a deafening whoosh and roar. All four missiles quickly reach their target, leaving a trail of smoke behind.

Cougar and Venom remained six miles away but spotted four flashes as each missile was launched in turn.

A cluster of four missiles soar through the air and are spotted in the distance by three jets.

Trojan quickly gets on the radio and says, 'Heads up. In coming. Razor and Pulsa get ready.'

Razor takes the lead and says, 'When they are within a mile, we split up and take on a missile each. Pulsa breaks left, Fox breaks right and I will pull up.'

They have mutually agreed and prepared to adhere to their instructions.

The three fighter jets heading towards the factory are targeted by four missiles hurtling through the air. To head towards them directly, they take a slight turn.

The four missiles are chasing the three pilots, and they follow the plan by having Pulsa go left, Fox go right, and Razor climb steeply.

As the missile nears, Pulsa begins to zigzag.

Enigma twists his neck to stare behind him and says, 'Whatever your plan, I suggest you do it now. It comes fast.'

Pulsa continues to make wide zig zags and says, 'When I come out of this slip and slide, I'll yank the stick and pull up. When I do, push the button.'

While flying from side to side, Enigma experiences the G force and is then thrust back as Pulsa makes the fighter jet, climb at a steep angle.

When he flies almost vertically, he quickly hits the button to deploy counter measures.

Bright yellow sparkling flares under the carriage disperse in a V shape, causing a huge explosion when the missile hits them.

One missile down, three more to go.

Razor has changed its course and is currently plummeting towards the ground with the *S-75 Dvinawill* in tow. He screams to deploy the flares. Continuing his steep fall, he flies to the left as an explosion and loud bang sound from behind.

Delta is relieved and says, 'That was close. We're outta here.'

Fox currently has two missiles pursuing him, but he has managed to lose them temporarily. As they near, they move in a side-winding motion.

Only one of the two missiles was destroyed despite the first burst of flares being set. The last missiles is still chasing Fox and Lobster.

Lobster gets jittery and says, 'That was too close. Firing another round of counter measures.'

The third burst is discharged, and ultimately destroys the last missile.

Fox gives a huge sigh of relief and says, 'You're clear to go Condor one and two.'

Cougar requests they go back to the boat and says, 'Great work. Head home. Will see you on the other side.'

Venom seconds that and says, 'Get outta here. Supersonic.'

The six pilots respond to the command without needing to be told again and increase their speed to the maximum.

Cougar and Venom are the only ones close by, and they don't know that *Chengdu J-20's* fighter jets are incoming. With full throttle and in attack formation, they execute their attack run. Both are eager to complete the mission and return home.

Cougar sets her aim on the doors and maintains her composure to ensure a precise hit. While attempting to lay up her attack, she's alerted by a warning sound and flashing light signaling a threat.

Storm stares at his radar and says, 'We have two bandits. Three o'clock.'

Cougar, being frustrated, says, 'Taking evasive action.'

She makes a hard right turn to confront the bandits and pass them on either side.

Venom is alerted simultaneously and mimics her.

Cougar gets on the comms and says, 'Venom. We can't complete our mission until we get rid of them.'

Venom copies and says, 'We go after the same one and shake them down.'

Cougar was thinking the same and says, 'With yah. Follow my lead.'

The two *Chengdu J-20's* pass their enemy and quickly maneuver to pursue the two jets.

Once Cougar is in a superior position, their threats break away left and right. She sees the one flank left and pursues them.

Cougar turns on her guns when she realizes she's too close to the *Chengdu J-20*, and fires after acquiring a target lock. The *Chengdu J-20* narrowly escapes a trail of flying bullets. The pilot pulls up with Cougar hot on its trail and Venom as backup.

The second Chengdu J-20 is turning around to assist his partner.

Venom knows what the pilot is going to do and says, 'He's coming round. We haven't got long.'

Cougar tries to get another tone and says, 'Almost there.'

Once she hears the tone, she shoots her guns and clips the wing of the *Chengdu J-20*. But its not enough to force it down.

Venom thinks he's got a clear shot and says, 'I can make a shot. When I say break left, I'll make the shot.'

Cougar has faith and says, 'Give me the signal.'

Venom is far enough to fire a missile and waits for a tone when he says, 'Break left.'

Cougar throws her arm to the left, allowing him a clear shot. A missile launched by Venom hits the *Chengdu J-20*, causing it to crash seconds later. They both scream with delight.

Soon after a victory, Venom fighter jet sends a warning of being targeted.

Trojan gives his concerns, saying, 'They have a lock on us. We need to shake em.'

Venom tries to think of a way to shake them and says, 'We can't out run them. Prepare to eject.'

A missile is fired by the *Chengdu J-20* fighter pilot after getting a tone.

At the moment Venom and Trojan were about to eject, Cougar unexpectedly emerges from above. Above them, they Cougar deploy her counter measures. The missile's explosion gives them time. Another missile is launched and strikes the Cougar jet, resulting in the aircraft being severed in two.

After pulling away from the explosion, Venom instinctively chases the *Chengdu J-20* and climbs on top of it. He shoots at them in a fit of anger. After that, he takes aim to fire a missile. The moment the tone turns into a repetitive beep, he presses the button and the missile hits its target directly.

Trojan gets on the comms to the ship and says, 'Condor one is down. I repeat, Condor one is down. Mission is unsuccessful. I repeat mission is a fail. We are out of missiles to complete the mission.'

The atmosphere in the Combat Information Center is tense and anxious, with everyone unsure if two of their colleagues have perished. Awaiting update from Condor two.

Buzz Saw prays to God for their survival.

From underneath, Venom and Trojan were unable to confirm if Cougar and Storm had escaped the explosion unscathed. They couldn't see anything due to the smoke and fire.

They look for them on the ground by making a pass, but they are not able to find them.

Buzz Saw wants them to return before more *Chengdu J-20* planes arrive in the vicinity..

Without any indication of a new threat, Venom flies back to the ship and a somber moment sets in the sky. Reflecting on the event and imagining a better outcome.

Its Not Over

The coastal area is being approached by Condor three, four, and five, which are being monitored by the comms officer. She confirms that Condor two is on its way too. Buzz Saw reflects on how Cougar suffered the same destiny as her fathers. He cannot shake the feeling that it was meant to be.

Buzz Saw solemnly says, 'Get them back safely. It wasn't supposed to be.'

Silence fills the room as no one finds anything worth saying.

The factory alarm is switched off, and the workers return to work. The supersonic jet is being readied for its fifth test run, with two pilots preparing to fly in the changing area.

If the test run is successful, it will be rolled out and initially released to Russia, Dubai, and Brunei.

The in-flight equipment inside the jet will be believed to have been developed first by China, while American technology will be exposed.

Eventually, Condor three, four, and five cross the East China Sea and bank right towards the *Philippine Sea*. Losing two of their own and failing to complete the mission has left them feeling deflated.

The four *F/A-18F Super Hornets* are almost there as Condor two finally catches up with them and the aircraft carrier is in sight. It's visible from about five miles away.

A man in a full flight suit with his helmet still on is lying a few miles away from the factory. As the plane went up in smoke, Storm managed to eject himself. The pluming black smoke concealed his ejection as the fighter jet slowly disintegrated.

The thick smoke made him pass out and he fell unconscious. He regains consciousness and questions his location and status. He lies on the ground and rolls onto his back to check if his surroundings are real.

He breathes a sigh of relief before worrying about his location and how he'll return to the carrier. The second thing on his mind is the whereabouts of his co-pilot.

After taking a quick look, Storm rises and scans the area for Cougar's landing, hoping to get lucky and spot her.

He scans his surroundings and notices a tiny dot in the distance that matches the color of his pilot uniform. Running closer, he hopes to get a better view and confirm if it is a Cougar. He moves closer with hope, trying to get a better view of the color and object, thinking it might be her.

He occasionally scans his surroundings for any dangers and peers up at the sky to watch for *Chengdu J-20* jets.

At a distance of one foot, he expresses relief upon realizing it's a Cougar. As he sees her lying face down, he carefully turns her over to check for vital signs. With his ear close to her mouth, he hears a faint breath. Feeling even more relieved now.

Cougar stirs awake slowly and startles after seeing Storm's face so close to hers, having briefly forgotten her location. She winces because of pain in her abdomen and examines for any wound. Similar to Storm, she ponders if they're in imminent peril and recognizes they're stranded in the wilderness.

As far as their eyes can see, there's nothing but miles of flat plain. It resembles a patchwork quilt without any farmers around. The temperature is moderately warm with cloudy gray skies.

With no civilization or communication methods, they're unsure how to get back home.

The cockpit seats cannot be located, for them to use the signal to be rescued.

Cougar is considering the possibility of scouring the fields for transportation. As she gathers her thoughts, she notices the factory in the distance.

Storm converses with her and says, 'I think we should walk east and hope we find help with the local native.'

Cougar has other ideas and says, 'I don't want to end up like my father and die out here. The factory is in the distance. I think we should find something driveable and steal it. Then find a way of getting picked up by helicopter.'

Storm kind of had the same idea as a second thought but as a last resort and says, 'After the chaos we caused, the factory security protection will probably be doubled.'

Cougar ponders on the two options available and says, 'Our only chance of making it home is finding some sort of transport at the factory. We have no food or water. We could be walking for days.'

Storm begrudgingly begins to agree and asks, 'Well, what are we waiting for? Let's go.'

They sauntered towards the factory, arriving at the outskirts of the site after half an hour.

To stay hidden, they crouch in the tall grass. They are watching the soldiers come and go inside the building from a distance of about forty feet.

Their view is from the side of the building, so they cannot see inside.

Storm begins to have doubts and says, 'I don't think we thought this through properly. I can't see any vacant vehicle to take. And without being seen.'

Cougar has another idea and says, 'The mission was clearly a fail. The building is intact and our people are no where to be seen in the sky. We can't let them go ahead with selling our technology.'

Storm wonders if she is thinking what he guesses and says, 'You're not thinking of stealing the plane.'

Cougar observes a way of getting past the soldiers and says, 'Yes. We either try to blow it up ourselves with what we can find or fly it out of here. What is your idea?'

Storm struggles to come up with anything and says, 'We kill two birds with one stone. Go home and stop them going through with their plan to sell American secrets.'

An unattended fire exit door is located on the side of the building. That's their way in. They take the opportunity to approach the door without being seen.

Cougar sprints towards the door while Storm trails close behind. They need to jar the door open to enter now. They fear encountering hostility once they open the door.

After wedging the door open, they enter and realize they're in the changing room. The sound of showers and heavy mist fill the air.

The cover is ideal for avoiding detection and not being patrolled.

Storm restrains Cougar by the shoulder and opens the door silently to peek through.

The entrance will take them straight into the hangar, where they'll be able to see the jet without their view being obscured.

Their native language and accent are detectable through the indistinct chatter. Naturally, not understanding what they're saying.

Cougar nudges her head outside from under his arm. Then closes the door quickly to avoid being seen by the staff in white coats or soldiers in a dark beige uniform.

Two pilot suits are hanging on the wall they passed on the way to the changing room door, and they both notice them.

The people in the shower must have finished flying the prototype or are about to. Upon checking their own flight suit, they realize that it's a completely different color than theirs. Their suits are gray while the test pilot suits are black. Therefore, they make the decision to exchange their clothing for the test pilot suits.

They're similar in size to Storms but slightly too big for Cougar. Her worry is that the people in the hangar will notice that something is off if she looks silly in the suit.

They both take off their suits in front of each other, revealing rubber-lined exposure suits underneath. So, they don't have to worry about revealing underwear or embarrassing clothing.

The showers stop and fail to remember there were people using them as they finish changing. Presuming they are the test pilots.

Cougar and Storm quickly hide their old suits..

The plan is to walk out confidently, approach the supersonic jet casually, and take off. Without arousing suspicion.

By wearing helmets with visors down, they conceal their face and prevent anyone from realizing they are not the real pilots. They're both perspiring within their helmets, anxious about being discovered.

Their breathing sounds like it's coming through a snorkel as if they're underwater.

For now, everyone is preoccupied with their own tasks in the hangar.

Cougar and Storm come face to face with the jet for the first time. As they walked under the wingspan, they were enveloped in the aura of the black aircraft.

They've almost made it to the cockpit without being questioned. The ladder that's stored below the cockpit is out. There are steel flat spikes on both sides of the square-shaped pole that you can step on.

Cougar climbs up first to get into the front seat. Storm then follows and gets into the back seat. Things are looking good so far.

The cockpit is typical of a fighter aircraft. There's no need for English labeling on the instruments.

In front of Storm, there is a medium-sized radar and several switches on either side.. The black glass gives the screen a state-of-the-art appearance.

Figuring out how to turn on the instrument panel takes a few seconds. The layout is similar to the F/A-18F Super Hornets as it is American technology. Although, with more sophisticated gadgets.

Storm wonders what she is doing about getting them out of here and says, 'Speak to me, Cougar. Can you fly this thing or not?'

Cougar hears the engine come on soon after he finishes his conversation and says, 'Getting there. Familiarizing yourself back there?'

Storm surprises himself with how quickly he is getting to grips with the controls and says, 'This was made for me. We have everything. Reverse missiles, reverse camera and a radar which can scan the skies for twenty miles.'

She is self-assured about piloting the jet and there have been no issues yet.

The two test pilots noticed the airplane engines humming and raised an alarm they realized their flight suit was missing. The plane has a unique and distinctive sound.

The turbines' rotation is inaudible due to a low humming sound.

The airplane is being enclosed by soldiers, following orders.

Guns are pointed at Cougar and Storm, alarming them. They seemed to have appeared out of nowhere. Although surrounded, the plane can safely reach the airstrip ahead without harming the soldiers.

A problem has emerged with an arm truck driving towards them with additional soldiers.

Cougar mentally determines the distance required to achieve take off speed and the distance between them and the truck approaching.

Storm becomes naturally agitated and says, 'Move it or lose it.'

Cougar remembers the lectures and says, 'Don't worry. She's bullet proof. Hang on. This is going to be tight. It's all or nothing.'

The afterburners engage and a burst of blue and yellow light emits from the plane's rear. The equipment behind the jets is scorched and the personnel are blown off their feet by the power of the jets.

As Cougar gently pulls the throttle to exit the hangar, the plane slowly pulls away. The jet's skin and canopy glass are hit by ricocheting bullets. The plane remains unmarked.

Cougar pushes the throttle to the max once they're clear of the building. The jet rapidly accelerates as the engine's power pushes them back into their seats.

Cougar is amazed at the plane's power and how it quickly approaches the truck. If she doesn't pull the stick back fast, they'll hit it.

She closes her eyes and wrestles with the control stick in her hand, fearing a crash during takeoff.

The top windscreen narrowly avoids being smashed by the front wheels as the driver shuts his eyes and slams on the brakes.

With the plane taking off, Cougar opens her eyes to see that they made it. She turned around swiftly and caught a glimpse of the truck being flipped through the air by the plane's powerful afterburners. The truck was knocked off its wheels by the strong airflow.

Realizing what happened, Cougar can't help but smirk.

Relief

As the jet climbs, it's moving further into the distance. Those on the ground at the factory can still observe the jet escaping.

The mission was to destroy the plane, which would indirectly destroy the factory, but they forgot. Cougar requests Storm to locate a method for triggering the back missiles. Storm figures out how to fire and aim at the target.

By clicking a few buttons, the rear camera is activated and an aiming target appears. By centering the building in the target system, Storm is able to press the firing button.

Smoke trails behind a bright light as it departs from the back of the plane and moves towards the building.

The people are able to witness the missile slowly approaching them. The workers and soldiers have enough time to flee the building. As the people distance themselves by twenty feet, the missile hits the building and the force of the explosion propels them far from harm.

Despite losing hope, Cougar and Storm successfully finished the mission. The next challenge will be to make it back to the boat.

Storm quickly discovers their flight direction and sets a path to return home. He's surprised at how great the equipment is.

Storm expects the co-ordinates to come on her screen in front of her and says, 'This thing is cool. I've just popped up a map of the terrain and a route to get us back to the boat.'

Cougar is impressed and says, 'Great. Nice work. Changing direction now.'

Storm sees if there are any bandits and says, 'Right. It looks like the coast is clear all the way home. This jet has everything. Except for a microwave.'

Cougar moves the throttle further forward to push the jet to go fast and says, 'We're outta here. Going hot and fast.'

Storm sees how long till they reach their destination and says, 'The route planner gives us an eta of one hour. At the speed we're traveling at.'

Cougar listens as she wonders about contacting base and says, 'Great. Now switch on the ESAT. So, they can spot us on the in the air. And get hold of the carrier.'

Storm plugs in his ESAT to the on board communication hardware then twists the dial and says, 'Connected and turned on.'

Cougar wants him to get in touch with their people and says, 'Great. Try to contact the boat.'

The comms officer is observing the four jets and sees that they are almost home. The loss of both the mission and their own has left everyone in a state of recovery..

The atmosphere is solemn, with the only audible noise being the comms officer's periodic reports on their position.

Suddenly, a blip appears on the radar. The comms officer is surprised when they immediately recognize the signal.

Buzz Saw notices their expression and asks, 'Is there a problem?'

Comms officer does not show conviction when he says, 'It's Storm. His ESAT has come on. It wasn't there a minute ago.'

Buzz Saw assumes there is a mistake and says, 'It could be glitch. Check again.'

Comms Officer continues to question himself and says, 'It says it's him. He's going hypersonic.'

Buzz Saw thinks out loud and says, 'He's airborne. But in what?'

The communication room now has a more positive atmosphere.

The radio emits a squawk and the comms officer requests confirmation of their status. They quickly came to the realization that it was Storm.

Comms officer reaches out. 'Storm. This is sea bird. Do you read?'

There is no response.

Comms officer repeats himself. 'This is sea bird. Do read Storm?'

Silence continues to fill the space.

Storm finally responds. 'This is Storm. Figuring out the comms still. Our arrival is in forty-five minutes.'

Buzz Saw asks, 'Where is Cougar? Is Cougar with you?'

Storm sounds happy and says, 'Yes. I repeat, Cougar is here. Both in one piece.'

Buzz Saw is curious to how they made it and asks, 'How are you traveling?'

Storm goes quiet at first and finally says, 'We found a plane we could fly.'

Buzz Saw is curious to what they are traveling in and asks, 'If you don't mind me asking, in what?'

There's a momentary silence.

Cougar comes on and says, 'We are traveling in the plane you wanted us to destroy. We failed to blow it up, so we took it.'

Everyone in the communication room quietly laugh except for Buzz Saw.

Buzz Saw cannot believe what he is hearing and says, 'You're to blow up the prototype. What about the factory?'

Cougar does not hesitate to say, 'Factory destroyed.'

Buzz Saw is relieved and falls back against a station and says, 'We all thought you were dead. And there was no chance of completing the mission with little ammunition.'

Waiting for a response, a red light inside the cockpit flashes, indicating low fuel.

The fuel warning light's appearance distracts Cougar, making her realize there isn't enough fuel to maintain hypersonic. It seems that the jet was not refueled, leaving a quarter of the tank empty.

They should be able to make it home, as long as they don't fly too fast.

She loses track of her conversation with Buzz Saw as she focuses on the instruments.

Cougar resumes communication and says, 'There is enough fuel to just about get us back. So, we have had to switch off the hypersonic.'

Buzz Saw considers refueling in midair and says, 'Unfortunately, we have no one in the vicinity who can gas you up. So, take it easy. We have you in our sight.'

Communication ends as there is nothing else to say.

The flight seems longer due to the silence while they are still half an hour from the carrier. They engage in small talk to make time pass quickly.

Cougar is interested in his plans when they get back to *Fallon* and asks, 'Is there anyone of interest you're dating?'

Storm has a number of women in his life and says, 'Nah. I'm not ready to settle down yet. Just like going out with different women.'

Cougar thinks he is wasting his life away and says, 'From my own experience, life is too short. Unless the women know you are dating them all and are fine with it, you should let them know. Tell them you have no interest in settling down with them. Find out if they still want to date you.'

Storm smiles and wonders why she is interested in his love life when he says, 'I didn't know you cared about my personal life. What about you? I noticed you had a picture of him which went up in smoke. Are you going to see him again?'

Cougar cannot wait to see him again and says, 'I hope so. We are still not out of the woods. A few miles before head to sea.'

Storm wonders what her feelings are towards Ethan and asks, 'Are you in love with him?'

Cougar struggles with her emotions to determine what they are and says, 'I've never been in love. I wouldn't have a clue.'

Storm doesn't believe her and says, 'You know if you are in love with him. It can be the first time with him.'

Cougar has no idea to determine and says, 'I know I really like him. I want to be with him right now. Thats all I know.'

Storm tests her to find out and asks, 'Would you marry him if he asked you to?'

Cougar doesn't have to think and says, 'Of course I would.'

Storm rolls his eyes and says, 'Then you are in love with him. Would you give up your job for him?'

Cougar has been wondering how to juggle her work between *Fallon* and Los Angeles and says, 'I've reached where I want to be as an aviator. There is nothing else I want to achieve. So, obviously I would choose him over my career.'

Storm gets frustrated and says, 'Well, you are in love with him. If you weren't, all that would be on your mind would work. Your career. But you have found something that is worth more than a career.'

Cougar still does not believe they are a measure of love and says, 'Anyone can give up a career for a friend or family. Anyone would say yes to marriage.'

Storm has another way of proving her feelings and asks, 'Would you let him fall in love with another woman or fight for him?'

Cougar doesn't give it another thought and says, 'Just thinking about it hurts. I could never let him go and see him with another woman. That would hurt like hell.'

Storm has now proved his point and says, 'That is how I know the women I'm dating don't care if I'm seeing other people. If they cared, they would order me not to see other women. And you would do anything to stop Ethan from looking at another woman. That is not caring for someone. That is, being in love. If you cared about his feelings, you would let him go. But you would fight for him, which goes beyond caring about his happiness.'

Cougar struggles to argue his point and has an epiphany as she says, 'Thinking of him with another woman makes me feel sick. I guess I am in love. Wow, I'm in love.'

Storm interrupts as he spots bandits on the radar and says, 'Sorry to interrupt your realization, but we have company. Two *Chengdu J-20*.'

Cougar thought about outrunning the two fighter jets by putting the jet in hypersonic, but then remembered they were low on fuel. It dawns on her that she'll have to engage in air-to-air combat. A dog fight to all the way home.

Two jets have arrived and can be seen at three and nine o'clock.

Cougar stares either side at the two pilots and says, 'We can't outrun them. We do not have enough fuel to go hypersonic. So, we have to lose them. Any ideas?'

Storm has to think for a minute and says, 'This jet is the best in the world. We don't need speed. We use it or lose it.'

Cougar checks what weapons are on the plane and then says, 'We have plenty of bullets and plenty of missiles. I'm going to use the guns.'

The pilot to their right creates hand gestures by making a fist and pointing their thumb downwards. Demanding to land. They are naturally ignored by Cougar and Storm.

Cougar has an idea and says, 'I'm going to do a death roll and make it difficult for them to fire at us. I'm going to count to three, then make her roll over on our left.'

Storm has no idea why she wants to fly over them and says, 'Whatever you think will work, go for it. I'm ready.'

Cougar begins to count and says, 'One...two...three.'

She performs a risky maneuver and flies upside down, facing the enemy. Storm is uncertain about her plans but watches it unfold.

The pilot of the *Chengdu J-20 fighter* is uncertain of what to do and is aware that his wingman is unable to make a move. Cougar waits patiently as they continue flying upside down, anticipating their next move.

They hesitate for a moment before panicking and attempting to escape. In response to watching their move, she spins into a vertical death roll.

She executed her plan perfectly, leaving no chance for the other fighter jet to make a safe shot.

Storm shuts his eyes to avoid getting dizzy and wishes the ride would end soon.

Cougar feels confident and says, 'Come on. Come on. Thats it. Whatever you can do, I can do better.'

Storm wonders how long she will keep this up for and says, 'I'm getting a headache. Now I know why you're the best.'

Cougar keeps her nerve and confidence as she says, 'Waiting for them to slip up so I can make a move. Another a few minutes and I got them.'

Eventually, the *Chengdu J-20* fighter pilot panics and attempts to pull away. After witnessing the fighter jet's departure, Cougar recovers from the death roll and activates the targeting system. The other pilot is having difficulty maintaining control of the aircraft. This allows her to get a tone. Then open fire with the machine gun. Losing control of the plane, the pilot ejects.

One down, one to go.

While Cougar watches for the other fighter jet, Storm monitors the radar for Chengdu J-20.

Warning lights come on while searching, making them a target. The rear camera turns on and Storm can see where the bandit is.

Cougar wants to know if he has a lock on them and asks, 'Can you see where the last fighter jet is?'

Storm has a clear view and says, 'See it. Right behind us.'

The plane maneuvers to evade the bullets coming its way. A couple clipped the left wing, but the bullet proof skin protected it from damage.

She rolls the plane to avoid more hits as bullets continue to fire.

The reverse missiles they fired slip their minds and they're not considering using them. She attempts to break right to get behind them, but they are skilled.

Cougar finally remembers about the weapons behind the plane and says, 'Storm. Use the rear missiles to knock them out.'

Storm does not need telling twice and says, 'Bear with me. Hold her steady. Need to get a lock.'

She tries to keep the jet steady while avoiding hails of bullets. While Storm tries to make a lock on the *Chengdu J-20,* another tone comes on.

Cougar is making them a sitting duck while allowing Storm to make a lock. She is not sure how much longer she can continue to stay on the present course and avoid getting hit.

Storm is close to getting a tone and says, 'Not much longer now. Steady. Steady. Got a lock.'

Switching to missiles, the *Chengdu J-20* goes to make another tone.

Cougar begins to panic and says, 'Hurry up. He is going to have a lock on us.'

Storm continues to get a tone and says, 'Any second now.'

Upon hearing a tone, the cougar prepares for a missile strike.

A missile launches and is on course for a direct hit. Shortly thereafter, Storm obtains a tone and fires a missile behind them.

As soon as Storm tells her he fired, Cougar breaks right. They hear a massive explosion and initially think it's them, but then realize they're still present. The *Chengdu J-20* was taken out.

She makes sharp turns left and right to lose the missile.

Losing it is a challenge, and her only option is to attempt hypersonic speed and risk fuel depletion.

She waits until she's flying straight and then increases the throttle to achieve hypersonic speeds. As the jet zooms off, the Cougar and Storm feel their bodies get pushed into the back seat. The missile was outpaced, allowing them to return home.

Pam slows down to conserve fuel as soon as the coast is clear and notices the indicator displays fuel almost empty. She hopes they will make it back to the carrier.

The engines stutter and show signs of malfunction. The moment they saw the aircraft carrier in the distance was perfect timing. Eventually, one of the engines gives out and cuts off.

Both of them are concerned about not surviving and contemplate ejecting, only to wait for the ship to collect them.

The comms officer in the communication room reports being less than a mile out and provides a commentary on their position. After a sigh of relief, Buzz Saw goes to make contact.

Cougar hears them and says, 'We are glad to see you. You have never looked so good.'

Storm gives a warning when he says, 'We've lost an engine and running on fumes.'

The second engine failure leaves them flying aimlessly in the wind.

Cougar gives the bad news when she says, 'Now engine two gone. We only have one chance to land. If we fail, we will have to eject.'

Buzz Saw raises the alarm for an emergency landing and says, 'We are preparing for your landing. They will be ready for you.'

As they descend, the cougar keeps the nose up, hoping for favorable winds.

She's struggling to keep the jet stable as they approach only a hundred yards away. She operates the switch to deploy the landing wheels.

Storm believes in her ability to take them to safety.

Cougar talks to herself and says, 'Come on. We've made it this far to suddenly die. Storm, prepare to eject if this goes south.'

Storm's finger hovers over the ejection button, hoping he won't have to use it.

The aircraft appears huge now that they are only a few feet away. As it comes in for landing, the jet sways a little from side to side.

A loud bang is heard as the wheels make contact with the deck and are subsequently caught by the net. They made it.

The plane made a safe landing. Cougar can't believe they made it on fumes. She has to pause and absorb all of it.

It's hard for Storm to believe what they went through and they're pondering how they made it.

I Gotta See About A Guy

♥

The pilots were greeted on the deck by everyone for making it home and completing the mission. Cougar is overwhelmed by the huge welcome as she stands inside the cockpit.

Storm is laughing and having fun during the celebration.

As they exit the plane, their friends and colleagues cheer and embrace them both. They are hoisted onto shoulders and displayed for all to see.

Everyone is joining in the celebration.

Buzz Saw chooses to stay away from the crowd, watching the momentous occasion outside the bridge, relieved that they made it back unharmed.

Buzz Saw catches the attention of Cougar and she briefly interrupts her celebration to glance up at him. He nods at her with a faint smile of approval. With a similar gesture, she reciprocates and returns to the celebrations with a smile.

A professional photographer takes several pictures of the scene, and one of the moments captured shows Cougar and Storm facing each other while holding arms.

After two days, the pilots returned to *Fallon Station* and were provided with additional papers for deployment. They're all heading back to their original station or aircraft carrier. Cougar is staying in *Fallon* since it's her hometown.

Yesterday, there was a farewell gathering at her uncle's bar.

Following her commendation for bravery and outstanding achievement, she will meet with Buzz Saw to talk about her future.

Cougar is anxious while waiting outside his office, curious about the purpose of the meeting. She hopes to not receive papers that will take her millions of miles away from Los Angeles. She has clammy hands and can't stop fidgeting with them.

She is eventually called in and stands before his desk, awaiting instructions.

Buzz Saw is sat back in his chair and appears lost for words until he eventually says, 'I spoke to the powers that be and they said you can have any duty of your choice.'

Cougar has a puzzled expression and says, 'I don't know what that means.'

Buzz Saw sighs as he collects his thoughts and says, 'You have any duty of your choice. Which means you can go anywhere you like.'

Cougar's mind goes blank and not sure how to respond as she says, 'I'm not sure what post to take. I thought I would ask for leave.'

Buzz Saw reads her mind and asks, 'You want to see my best friend? See what the outcome is before you decide.'

Cougar feels strange admitting to choosing love over her career and says, 'Yes sir.'

Buzz Saw is open and frank as he says, 'I thought you were dead. I imagined you went down the same way as your father. But, when I heard your voice, I was relieved. Thought you were a ghost. When you face death, it evaluates your life. When you are around our age, you start to think about what is more important. You've given enough of your life to the Navy. You question what life is about. So, I'm calling you out. You want to see if Ethan is worth fighting for. Him over furthering your career.'

Cougar is not sure how to articulate her feelings and says, 'It feels a bit childish putting love before an important role. Where the lives of others depend on you. I really want to see him. But, I have had a few days to get a reality check. His true one love died. I will be a second choice. Right.'

Buzz Saw does not show any emotion or show suggestive choice and says, 'Forget about your fellow men. It is just us here. You don't have to justify anything. What is it you want? A chance of happiness or give it up for something you already know what the outcome is. Is your next move going to be better than something you have a chance to explore? Your job will be here. It is not going anywhere.'

Cougar now sees her dilemma more simplified and says, 'I cannot stop thinking about him. He makes me want to get out of bed every day. He is the missing puzzle in my life. Sir.'

Buzz Saw does not smile or show joy once and says, 'Go. Take leave. Say a month. If you think he is worth it, you decide your duty around that. You've earned it.'

Cougar is torn between jumping for joy inside or maintaining a professional demeanor. However, she was advised to encourage her to pursue Ethan.

It felt strange to not go back to work and instead stay at home, where I had the time to make changes to the house and donate my late wife's clothes to charity. Moving forward and only holding onto memories in photographs.

I removed all my power suits from my wardrobe and now only have casual clothes I purchased in Las Vegas, along with some additional items.

Lately, I've been using my spare time to cook and try new recipes that I found through my cell phone internet searches.

My daughters sometimes call me for reassurance before making business decisions. They call me while I'm cooking or reading to pass the time between my engagements.

I've also been getting my nails done and enjoying massages.

Pam has been on my mind since she left and I wondered if she made it home. My mind has been consumed by thoughts of our relationship and intimacy. It seems like I'm in mourning for her and she's never coming back.

The memory of going to Las Vegas for dinner, and being flown there by her, remains vivid. The time I met her family and the near-death experience on the way back.

Keeping myself occupied is how I deal with things. It's been helpful to avoid constantly checking my phone for her messages.

I'm constantly thinking about our last night together and trying to remember every little thing. I recall how amazing her scent was and how stunning she looked. Recalling the scent of her perfume and the outfit she was wearing. I often think back to how her hair was and how she was such a great kisser.

In my mind, I remember how amazing her body was and how she tasted.

While chopping vegetables for an early dinner on a Thursday, my mind wanders to Pam once more. On a table stand, my tablet is being used to follow a recipe.

I have casual trousers on and my shirt sleeves are partially rolled up. A bottle of Rose has been opened and poured. While getting the ingredients ready, I enjoyed a cold, crisp, fruity flavor.

The kitchen's bifold doors offer a view of my garden. My garden is open and features randomly placed Greek-style statues.

Soft music is currently being played on one of my cell phone apps. Establishing a peaceful ambiance.

I'm in the middle of frying garlic with finely chopped onions when the doorbell interrupts me and I notice it's already four o'clock. I'm wondering who could be coming over so early without prior plans.

To prevent burning, I turn off the stove and remove the pan from the heat. I'm a little annoyed as I make my way to the door, feeling frustrated by the interruption.

As soon as I opened the door, I saw Pam standing there with a blank stare on her face. I'm caught off guard and curious about how she found my address. I expected her to inform me when she returned from the assignment, but I haven't received any news from her.

She pounces on me before I can gesture her in and express my excitement at seeing her in person. Our lips meet and she almost loses her balance. I reciprocated naturally, and a flood of memories came back.

We continued kissing as I guided us to the living room. Without a word, we collapse onto the couch with her beneath me.

Having her in my world and home feels strange since I've never discussed my life and living space.

Pam is reminded of how wonderful he smells and how skilled he is at kissing. She misses the way he holds her and stares into her eyes.

She has been eagerly anticipating this moment for over a week since returning from her trip to China. The unknown prospect of being held by him again.

They end up making love on the floor in the center of the room. Feeling impatient while waiting for the other person to undress completely.

Nearly two hours of giggling, making love, and discussing their recent activities left them both feeling drained as they sat up against the sofa.

We engage in small talk, ignoring the obvious issue of our emotions and future plans.

I'm curious to how she found me and ask, 'How did you know where I lived?'

Pam gazes into my eyes and says, 'Holden. You gave him your address.'

We eventually talk about what lies ahead.

Since our last meeting was our last, I need to determine where I stand with Pam. To avoid disappointment, we tend to assume the worst.

Pam wants to go first and mentions that she can't discuss the mission with me as she says, 'I have something to say. My plane got shot down and had no idea if I would make it out alive. The only thing which spurred me on was not seeing you again. It made me realize what strong feelings I have for you. I love you Ethan. I realize I loved you the moment I departed.'

I smile, knowing that is what I wanted to hear and say, 'I want you in my life, whether it is just as a girlfriend and boyfriend or something more. I don't want us to be apart again.'

Pam goes speechless realizing her surroundings and says, 'This is a big house. I pictured maybe a five-bedroom house. I want this too. What we have, but this world. It scares me. I never owned a house. Your living room was the same size as my house on base.'

I pick up on her past tense. and asks, 'Does that mean you have left *Fallon Station*?'

Pam shakes her head and says, 'I was given any choice of duty. I found that there was nothing else I need to prove to myself. Ended up making a choice between my future career in the middle of nowhere, alone, and you. This is what I want. I can find a pilot's job somewhere. Maybe become a flight instructor. Other than that, I'm jobless and have no idea.'

I feel excited about the future and say, 'Well, I quit my job. And I have no idea what I want to do. Except be with you. There is plenty of room here. I can show you around LA and go for coffee. There are more choices here than *Fallon*.'

Pam smiles, almost laughing, and says. 'I would like that. There is something I want to ask you.'

I'm not sure what it could be and say, 'Anything.'

Pam turns her body to face me and asks, 'Will you marry me? At some point in the future. It doesn't have to be now.'

I do not need to pause for thought responding before she can finish her sentence saying, 'Yes. I want to. I'm ready to move on.'

Our proposal leaves us speechless and we express our acceptance through a kiss.

Thank you so much for buying and reading my book!!

Can you please leave a STAR RATING? NO WRITTEN REVIEW REQUIRED

US:
http://www.amazon.com/review/create-review?&asin=B0B2X1J4Z4

CA:

http://www.amazon.ca/review/create-review?&asin=

UK:
https://www.amazon.co.uk/review/create-review?&asin=B0B2X1J4Z4

DE:

https://www.amazon.de/review/create-review?&asin=B0B2X1J4Z4

Subscribe for new future e-book releases below.

JOIN LEON M A EDWARDS MAILING LIST NOW

Sign Up Now to Join my official lists for consistent update about my books.

Subscribe

BOOKS ALSO BY LEON M A EDWARDS

Strangers To Lovers Tropes

Visit Leon M A Edwards Author Page On Amazon

Leon M A Edwards Amazon Author Page United Kingdom

Leon M A Edwards Amazon Author Page United States

Leon M A Edwards Amazon Author Page Canada

Free Book

Click Here

15 Great Books

Spy Thriller

Jane Knight Rogue Officer

Jane Knight Fair Game

Jane Knight A Spy Among Us

Jane Knight Tomorrows World

Romance

Blind Love Slow Burn

Blind Lover Short Version

To The Stars
By Chance

Second Chance

Six Weeks

Thriller

Ponta Delgada A Good Place To Die

Cold Bones

Paranormal

Eternity Wing And A Pray
Eternity Reassembly

About Author

I write in several genres, with the trope being strangers to lovers. You can learn more about me on the platforms below.

twitter.com/

tiktok.com/

instagram.com/

facebook.com/

amazon.com/

https://studio.youtube.com/

I would like to dedicate this book to Andrea, Alina and Lilia for leaving me to it, to write.

Acknowledgments

Thank God for giving me the confidence to start writing and the ability to write a story.

Published by Algenon Publication

www.leonmaedwards.com

Made in United States
Troutdale, OR
02/24/2024

17942684R00124